BROKEN BUTTERFLIES

Debra Lowry

Author's Tranquility Press

MARIETTA, GEORGIA

Debra Lowry /Publishing Company Name
Street Address
City, State/Province Postal-Code
www.website-url.com

Publisher's Note: This is a work of fiction. Names, characters, places, and incidents are a product of the author's imagination. Locales and public names are sometimes used for atmospheric purposes. Any resemblance to actual people, living or dead, or to businesses, companies, events, institutions, or locales is completely coincidental.

Broken Butterflies/ Debra Lowry
Paperback: ISBN 978-1-956480-58-0
E-book: ISBN 978-1-956480-59-7

This book is dedicated to my stepfather, Joe Van Nice. You inspired me to write this book, Joe - I love you. He has passed away now I wish he was still alive so he could see the finished product but it was all his idea.

Contents

Broken Butterflies

On the morning of February 7, 1992, Nicholas Wilson, a prominent tax attorney from one of Scottsdale Arizona's most affluent families, persuaded a judge to order a psychiatric evaluation of his ex-wife, Jessica Wilson. For years the couple had been in an ongoing, heated battle over financial matters and the custody of their two sons, Jayson and Brian. Nicholas Wilson told the judge that he was afraid that Jessica's anger was so intense that she might "do harm to herself or the children", that she was unstable and possibly dangerous. Nicholas said it reminded him of a "Fatal Attraction" scenario. Unfortunately for him, Nicholas Wilson was right. Seven hours after he was granted custody of his boys, he entered Jessica's home on Cactus Drive in Scottsdale and she shot him three times with a .357 Magnum. Six-year-old Jayson Wilson witnessed his father's slaying through a hole in a bedroom door where he and his younger brother were huddled in terror. The media was in a frenzy; not only was the case covered in the local news, it was also on Court TV and Entertainment Tonight. Jessica Wilson was charged with first-degree murder.

Her trial was the buzz of Scottsdale and the rest of the nation for two years. Jessica claimed that Nicholas had beaten her and verbally abused her for years; she claimed that she shot him in self-defense because he was "coming at her" with a knife. The prosecution argued that the knife had been placed in Nicholas's hand by Jessica herself.

Nicholas Wilson's seven brothers and sisters, all lawyers and doctors in Scottsdale, filled the front row behind the prosecutor. They watched with grim expressions as Jessica dramatically sobbed throughout the trial. Jayson Wilson testified that he thought he saw something "glary" in his father's hand. When Jessica was found "not guilty", most people in Scottsdale were surprised, many more were furious; some were simply mystified.

Jayson Wilson may have been the only witness that day and may have been trying to help his mother, who had a very manipulative and dysfunctional relationship with her boys. But there was someone else who watched the entire drama unfold . . . for days, months, even years, before it happened, someone who had a front row seat in Jessica's life. This woman was quiet and stayed in the background. She was afraid of the knowledge she had and was relieved that she was not forced to testify. Telling the truth would have put HER in danger. *I know, because that woman was me.*

CHAPTER ONE

Lighting Strikes

A scorching heat blasted the air on Friday afternoon as I sat in my silver Camry, watching kids trickle out of school, ants from an anthill, wearing their bright pastels and chattering like magpies. The air was so hot, even with the air-conditioning on full-blast, the inside of the car was an oven and my cotton dress stuck to my skin. As I glanced at my watch, my neck muscles tightened like wire. I had a dental appointment in fifteen minutes and the snippy receptionist had bitched at me the last time I was late, reminding me that the dentist was on a tight schedule. I wrinkled my nose. Screw her! I was on a tight schedule too and I never griped at her when I had to wait an hour, reading dusty old fishing magazines! I decided to give Trevor, my 6-year-old son, five more minutes to show up; after that I'd go in and corral him. Right now I needed to rest.

I turned on my favorite "Enya" cassette and leaned my head back. The soft, lilting music soothed my jangled nerves. I visualized myself resting comfortably on the plump, rose-colored sofa in my living room and I smiled inside, imagining the scent of a vanilla candle trickling into my nostrils like a brook bubbling into a thirsty stream, awakening my senses. Soon I was slipping sideways into a drowsy pink haze, far from the maddening crowd. Just at that precarious moment between wakefulness and bliss, a loud, demanding rap on my window burst my warm bubble, jolting me back into the cold water of reality. I felt ripped off, like I'd just heard someone scratching the needle on a record player across a vintage album.

Suddenly, an enormous bolt of heat lightning etched a jagged path across the sky. Against the blinding illumination, the silhouette of a woman appeared next to my car door, facing the window. She was a shadow with no eyes and no soul, a cardboard ghost that jumps out from nowhere on a scary carnival ride!

I shivered and sat up straight, trying to decide whether I should open the window or lock the door! A gnawing in my gut warned me to proceed with caution. Slowly, I lowered the glass barrier that protected me from the woman. As she came into view, my jaw dropped.

She was stunning. An expensive navy coatdress enhanced her tall, perfectly proportioned body. Thick, shiny brown hair was stylishly cut just above her shoulder blades and the bag she clutched reeked of elegance.

"Excuse me. My name is Jessica Wilson," she said. Her voice was husky and sensual, like that of a woman answering a 1-800 sex call.

"Hi. I'm Judy Kirkpatrick," I replied. I held out my hand. Her soft, perfectly manicured hand took mine. A strange current of energy flowed from her. It was surprisingly strong and also kind of weird and unsettling.

"I know who you are. I've been watching you." Her words were casual, as if she were giving me the time of day. I was fascinated by her poise but at the same time a bit paranoid.

"You have?"

"Yes. My son Jayson is in the same class as your son Trevor. Jayson's been dying to invite Trevor over to play. Several times I've been about to approach you but you rushed away."

"That sounds about right. I'm usually in a hurry." Something about her made me feel tingly and edgy, like the feeling I had when I met a new man I found attractive.

"Trevor told Jayson you've been sick." Concern showed in her face and she gently touched my arm.

"Yes . . . . I have Chronic Fatigue Syndrome." Tears stung my eyes.I had been struggling with the illness for two years and was often tired. Being a single mother added to the fatigue. Trevor never said anything about it to me, he never complained. When he saw me faltering, he would get me a pillow and blanket and urge me to lie down on the couch. I sometimes asked him if it bothered him and he would just tell me a joke in response. It surprised me that he had talked to Jayson about it and I wondered if he was more worried than he let on.

"That must be rough." she replied.

"It can be at times." With some people I tried to hide or downplay my condition but Jessica had such warm eyes, I felt I could just be myself.

"I have a friend who has it. She lost her job and her husband left her." Jessica quickly covered her mouth. "Judy, I'm sorry! That was rude of me!"

She looked so horrified I had to smile. "It's okay. I'm in a support group and I've heard some pretty grim stories. I'm doing pretty well. At least I can work four days a week."

"Well you certainly don't LOOK sick!" she said, her eyes sweeping my face as if she were memorizing it.

"Thanks." My neck was starting to hurt from looking up at her so I opened the door slightly, waiting for her to back up so I could get out. She stood there for a moment, staring at me intently, then stepped back just far enough for me to squeeze through a narrow opening. I flattened myself against the door. I was surprised to see the hint of pain in her green eyes. It was obvious that she had been crying but her make-up was still almost perfect. I was a little jealous; I always looked like a tomato-faced baby when I cried.

"Jessica, what's wrong?" I felt guilty. Here she had been so concerned about my health and she was obviously upset about something.

"I just found out my husband is having an affair with his secretary!" Her shoulders shook as she took out a tissue and began sobbing. "We've been married for eight years. God, I just feel sick!"

Instinctively I touched her arm. "You poor thing!" My heart sank as my thoughts flashed back to a day, several years previously, when I had rummaged under my car seat for a lost pen and found a cassette tape case full of women's names and phone numbers. My musician ex-husband had collected them while traveling with his rock band. I had been deeply hurt and enraged, especially since I was eight months pregnant at the time! Then I'd called each woman, pretending to be from the Health Control Center, to inform them that Rob had a venereal disease. "I've been through it myself. It stinks!" I felt a headache coming on just thinking about it.

"You have?" She shook her head. ".How could any man be foolish enough to cheat on YOU!" There it was again; it was almost like she was flirting with me.

I shrugged. "It happened a few months ago as a matter of fact. A man I was dating, Troy, swept into my life and dazzled me. Then he went to Club Med and I never heard from him again." I tried to keep my voice light but the truth was, the pain was still fresh.

I had truly thought Troy was my "soulmate" and my self-esteem had plummeted after the rejection.

Jessica shook her head and her eyes narrowed. "Men! They think they call all the shots! Bastards! What does Troy do for a living?"

The question threw me. I wondered what difference it made. "Actually he was a retired chiropractor."

"It's a shame you lost that one! At least you could have gotten some money from him!" She snorted.

"It's no loss." I lied, thinking of the nights I had been unable to sleep and the feeling of gravel churning in my stomach when I thought of Troy. But I realized Jessica was really hurting and I felt I should keep my misery to myself. "I'm sure there are some nice men out there Jessica. You're so beautiful. You'll have your pick of them, believe me!"

Her expression softened. "Thanks. You're sweet."

"It will take time. But eventually you won't hurt so much." At least that's what I was trying to convince myself.

"Well, I'm not letting him off easy! After all I've done for him. I gave him some of the best years of my life, gave him two beautiful boys. Believe me, he's going to be very sorry!" Her face sharpened into a grimace and she reminded me of J.R. on "Dallas" when he was about to confront a foe, eager, excited, like a hunter stalking his prey. I stepped back, feeling like an icy breeze had swept over me.

"What do you mean?"

"Oh, nothing." She smiled. "Please forgive me. I'm not myself today."

"You don't have to apologize Jessica. You need to talk to someone at a time like this. I'm flattered that you felt you could confide in me."

"Oh, I've had a good feeling about you. You have such a sweetness about you. I've been hoping we could become friends."

I was touched at her kindness. I could see the lonely little girl behind the mask of sophistication she wore. I smiled and squeezed her arm. "I'll pray for you."

She bit her lip. "Thanks. Please don't worry about me. I'm tougher than I look."

Jessica shielded her eyes with her hand to block the blinding sun. "I should get back to my car. Oh, look who's here!"

"Mom!" Trevor bounded up to me and gave me a bear hug. I inhaled the little-boy smell of sweat and dirt that I loved.

"Hi honey. How was school?" I automatically switched into my "mom" role, brushing back his thick, dark hair. He pulled away and made a face.

"Mom, stop it! You know I hate that! Hi Mrs. Wilson." Jessica's expression was almost angelic as she smiled at Trevor. "Hi kiddo. Did you play with Jayson at recess today?"

"Yep. We're gonna get together this weekend if it's okay with you Mom." He flashed his beautiful smile at me. He already had girls calling him. His self-confidence amazed me, since I still struggled with my own. I sometimes wondered where he'd gotten it.

"I'd love to have him over!" Jessica chirped. "I'll have lots of free time now since I've been dumped!" She laughed and winked at me. It was good to see she had a sense of humor. I knew it would help her right now.

"Sounds fine to me." I remembered my dental appointment. "I've got to go. Listen, let me give you my number. It's unlisted." I opened my purse to search for a pen. "Oh, I already have your number!" She waved and blew me a kiss and walked away grinning.

CHAPTER TWO

Girl Crush

The next day was Saturday. Trevor went to a friend's house to play so I had a quiet house. I was taking a "Screenwriting" class from the local community college and I had homework to do. I was writing the first ten pages of my script. I had been struggling for years to get some of my work published and was putting together a portfolio of poems, short stories and other projects I had labored over. I had majored in journalism in college but had ended up working at a series of secretarial jobs that paid the rent but never gave me any satisfaction. Writing was my passion and I was determined to keep at it, despite my busy job at a publishing firm, single parenting and my health issues. I dreamed of someday making it big. I constantly visualized myself walking across the stage to accept my Oscar at the Academy Awards. I even had my dress picked out, a slinky Venetian blue gown. Often I had to write amidst noise; the clanging of the garbage trucks outside my window, the blare of the television when Trevor was home, the annoying scraping of chairs I often heard from the condo above me. Today I was grateful for quiet, even though I missed Trevor.

I finished my assignment, put away the clean laundry, loaded the dishwasher, quickly ran the vacuum and made the beds. Then I put on my bikini and took a thick blue towel out to my balcony to sunbathe. I was on the 8th floor and I was fairly certain that no one could see me from the busy highway below but I still self-consciously sucked in my stomach as I smoothed on sunscreen. Then I settled myself comfortably, breathed a deep sigh of contentment and put on my headset with an "Eagles" cassette in it. As I hummed along with "Tequila Sunrise" I felt mellow and light, like I'd just seen a great movie. I started to drift off to sleep but an irritating noise kept intruding on my doze. Sighing, I took off the headset and heard the clatter of the telephone. Damn! I should have turned off the ringer. Reluctantly I got up and headed toward the kitchen phone.

"Hello". I spoke quietly, instantly deciding that I would make myself sound a little sick, so I wouldn't have to talk long. I hated talking on the phone since I did it all day at work.

"Judy? It's me. Jessica Wilson. Do you have a few minutes?" She sounded like she'd been crying again. I glanced at the sunny pool of light on my balcony where I'd left my daydreams and reluctantly sighed.

"Sure. How are you?"

"Dreadful. Nicholas moved out today. I'm a wreck!"

"Jessica, I'm sorry!" I leaned against the wall and slid down the side of it until I sat, Indian-style, on the cold kitchen floor. For an hour I listened to Jessica's saga. She told me she'd been married briefly in her 20s and had been a legal secretary in Minnesota for years. When her firm had opened an office in West Scottsdale, she had jumped at the chance they gave her to transfer to Arizona and had relocated to Scottsdale. In 1980, Jessica attended a party where she met Nicholas Wilson, a very successful real estate attorney. They eloped shortly after that. Nicholas was the oldest of eight children from a very affluent family in Scottsdale. He had graduated from Harvard, where he had been captain of the football team. His father, John Wilson Sr. was Scottsdale County's first neurosurgeon. Four of Nicholas's siblings became doctors and another sister became an attorney. One brother was a well-known artist and playwright in Scottsdale.

According to Jessica, Nicholas's family had disliked her from the start and often didn't invite her to family gatherings. In spite of their wealth, the family was stingy and Jessica had reluctantly continued working as a legal secretary during the first years of her marriage. After eight years of marriage and after giving Nicholas two beautiful sons, Jessica had recently followed him one night and caught him at a motel with his young, red-haired secretary. I thought

Nicholas must be an idiot since Jessica was one of the most beautiful women I'd ever met. Because Jessica opened up to me, I shared with her the details of my "Troy" situation. Candy, my friend and neighbor, had introduced us. From the moment I'd met him, I'd been infatuated. Blond, muscular, witty and intelligent, Troy listened to me and encouraged me with my writing. He had even hinted that he might be able to connect me with people who could help me get published. He'd been all over the world and I had lived a rather sheltered life so I was dazzled by him.

When he went to Club Med for a vacation, promising to stay in touch, I had written to him but got no response at all. One day at the swimming pool, Candy told me that Troy had met a 20 year-old flight attendant and was moving in with her! I was hurt and humiliated! When I shared my story with Jessica, she was so sympathetic and caring, I felt better than I had in months.

"Judy, I just don't get it," she sighed. "Troy would have been so lucky to have you. And I've tried so hard for years to be a good wife to Nicholas. Life just isn't fair, is it?"

"Sometimes it isn't," I replied. "Jessica, do you have family back in the Midwest? Are they supportive of you?"

She laughed hollowly. "No. My dad left us when I was little and my mom's crazy."

"Crazy? You mean she's mentally ill?"

"That's a nice way of putting it. Judy, I don't want to talk about her, okay?"

"Sure. I'm sorry Jessica." I felt sorry for her. I realized how lucky I was. I was the oldest of seven kids and had a close-knit, loving family. Jessica really didn't have anyone. I felt protective of her. She asked if Trevor and I would like to go to church with her and her boys on Sunday.

We'd been attending a Presbyterian Church off and on but I was on a spiritual quest of sorts and I was always open to trying new churches. Jessica gave me the address of the church and we made plans to meet there and then go to her house for lunch and a swim. I felt myself opening up to her more and more. The fact that she went to church indicated to me that she was trying to live a spiritual life.

After we hung up I went back outside but the sun had been covered by clouds. My shoulders slumped as I realized I had given her my precious time. But I consoled myself with the thought that I had helped someone who was in a difficult situation, someone who was rapidly becoming a friend. Besides, Jessica intrigued me. I felt like I was studying an exotic butterfly that had been batted out of the air by a bird of prey. I wanted to see the butterfly right itself, spread its' wings and fly again in all its' glory. But even more, I wanted to see HOW the butterfly did it! I had been batted down myself quite a few times and I felt like some of my colors had faded during the struggle. Maybe I would learn something from this creature.

Sunday dawned bright and clear. Trevor was jazzed about spending the day with the Wilsons. Jessica had told me that people dressed casually at her church so I wore a pink and white cotton dress with a matching sweater. She had also explained that the Scottsdale Community Church services were being held in a movie theater in Parkway Plaza which was only 10 minutes from my home. We parked in the crowded lot across from the theater and I was amazed at how many people were heading towards the front entrance. Jessica stood in the lobby, looking beautiful in a yellow linen dress and she beamed when she saw us and opened her arms to hug me.

"Judy! I'm so glad you made it!" As we embraced I inhaled her Chanel No. 5. At the same time I smelled stale popcorn from the nearby concession stand. "We're only meeting here temporarily," she said apologetically, as if she'd read my mind. We're trying to raise money for a new church building. Hopefully that will happen soon." She introduced me to her sons Jayson, who was 6 and had red hair and freckles, and Brian, a 4-yr-old with beautiful blond hair. They wore matching shirts. Trevor joined them and all three boys started giggling and whispering with each other.

There was a relaxed, friendly atmosphere that was much different from the rather stiff and formal church I had been attending lately. I already felt at home here. We trooped into one of the theaters and sat in the comfortable, plush maroon chairs that rocked back and forth. There was contemporary music being played by a group of young people and soon the entire room was packed. After the congregation sang two songs, a tall, lean man in his 30s with a shock of dirty blond hair bounded enthusiastically up to the podium and introduced himself as Pastor Luke. He gave a very upbeat and stimulating sermon about relationships in the 90s. To reinforce his point he showed a brief clip from one of my favorite movies, "When Harry Met Sally". I hung on to every word; with the stress I'd been through lately over Troy, I needed comfort and guidance. A pretty brunette woman named Christine sang "Amazing Grace" and tears welled in my eyes. Jessica whispered that Christine was a friend of hers and that the three of us should get together for dinner some night.

After the service, we joined everyone in the lobby where coffee and refreshments were being served. Pastor Luke stood outside the door, shaking hands with people as they left. Jessica and I stopped in front of him so she could introduce me.

"Pastor Luke, I'd like you to meet my friend Judy Kirkpatrick."

"It's nice to meet you Judy. Welcome!" Pastor Luke's handshake was firm. "Are you two sisters?"

Jessica giggled and shrugged her shoulders. "Maybe in some other lifetime!"

He shook his head. "It really is quite remarkable how much you two look alike! Judy please come back again."

"I plan to!" I assured him. He turned to the people behind us but I didn't want to leave. I'd found so much comfort here I didn't want to go back out into the sometimes heartless world. As we headed to the parking lot, with our boys tagging behind us, Jessica chattered about men. She remarked that she hoped she would meet someone new soon since it looked like her marriage was over.

"I'm picky!" She arched her eyebrows. "I'll only date handsome men, but money is the most important thing!" At first I felt uncomfortable at her remark; she sounded so cold and clinical. But then I thought maybe I should take a hint from her. I had a history of dating handsome, charming but mostly unemployed musicians and artists. Often I ended up paying for many of the dates we went on. I watched Jessica strut to her car and I was fascinated. She would be a good influence on me! We said our goodbyes and Jessica and her boys drove off to her house to make lunch for all of us. Trevor and I stopped to get gas and then headed towards Jessica's home, following the directions she had given me.

Jessica's home was quite impressive. It reminded me of a little stone castle, perched on the top of a hill overlooking a duck pond. The yard was meticulously arranged with hot pink hibiscus bushes circling a small cactus and rock garden. Yellow roses surrounded the front porch and a welcome mat made of straw was covered with sandals of various sizes. The front door was slightly open and as I was about to knock, I heard Jessica yelling at someone.

"Damn you Susie, put Nicholas on the phone right now!" Her voice was angry and menacing. "You lying bitch, I know he's there! Let me talk to him!"

Trevor and I looked at each other and shook our heads. "Let's just wait out here," I told him.

He nodded and we sat down on the front step. I was embarrassed and I didn't want to barge in, especially when she was so angry. I was surprised to hear her talking like that; the screaming woman I had just heard seemed so different from the one I'd just gone to church with. But I knew she was going through a tough time and I wondered if perhaps "Susie" was Nicholas's girlfriend. If so, I didn't blame Jessica for being furious.

"Your family is going to pay for this Susie, mark my words!" Her tirade continued as we sat there. "Your asshole brother owes me big time! Oh yeah? Well you can go straight to hell!" The phone was slammed down loudly. I decided to wait a few minutes, to let her calm down. Obviously she had been chewing out Nicholas's sister. I felt awkward and wondered if we should just leave. But I knew Trevor would be really disappointed if we didn't stay so I sighed and rang the doorbell.

"Hey you guys!" Jessica threw open the front door and waved us in. She wore a skimpy black bikini that revealed her abundant curves. As she stood in the sunlight, for a brief moment, she seemed to sway like an exotic dancer and I felt slightly uneasy, as if I had stumbled upon pornography hidden in someone's drawer. She acted like nothing was wrong so I figured she didn't want to talk about the phone call we'd just heard. She seemed so happy to see us I was touched. She ushered us in and I quickly scanned the house. The living room was sprawling and cool, with lots of chrome and glass furniture. She led us through sliding glass doors to the pool, which reminded me of one you might see in a luxury hotel, complete with all the colorful beach balls and floating air mattresses you could ask for. The Wilson boys were splashing each other and they yelled excitedly when they saw us. Trevor peeled off his t-shirt and jumped into the pool with them.

"He's so handsome. He looks exactly like you." Jessica watched Trevor for a few moments, seemingly lost in thought. For a brief moment I wondered why she kept staring at him. I shook my head, chiding myself for my paranoia.

"Well your boys are dolls too! They both have such gorgeous hair!" I replied.

She smiled wistfully. "I guess I have Nicholas to thank for that. He comes from a family of redheads and blonds. Me, I've always had this mousy hair."

"Mousy? Are you kidding?" I wondered if she was fishing for compliments or she really didn't get how stunning she was. "You have gorgeous hair."

Her eyes took on a dreamy glaze and she reached over and stroked the side of my hair. "Not like yours. Yours is like silk. Come with me." She grabbed my hand and led me down the hall to her bedroom. It had thick, white carpeting and the furniture was king-sized, painted white and gold. I felt like I was in a swanky hotel. She kept holding my hand until we reached a set of three-way mirrors. "Look." She turned me until I faced the mirrors and watched me carefully. I held my breath for a moment. My eyes met hers in the mirror; she was staring at me intently and a shiver went down my spine. "See Judy." She pointed at my reflection. I felt mesmerized and powerless to resist her orders. I looked at myself and saw a tall, slender woman with long brown hair, green eyes and an oval face tanned to light golden shade. Then I slowly slid my eyes back to Jessica's reflection. Although I surmised that she was a few years older than me and there were some tiny lines around her eyes, we could have been sisters. Even twin sisters! I realized I had seen this the first time I'd met her but had pushed it to the back of my mind. It was too unsettling.

I let out a long breath. "Wow!" I felt the need to lighten the situation, which was feeling heavy and somewhat surreal. She walked to the bed and sat down, then patted the place next to her. Her voice was soft and sensuous as she leaned back and stared at me. "I've been watching you for a couple of months. You remind me so much of myself when I was younger. So pretty, so sweet and vulnerable." She seemed to be lost in thought, almost as if she were talking to herself. "I was like you before all this happened to me. I wanted to talk to you the first time I saw you but I didn't want to scare you."

I walked over and sat down next to her. I saw for the first time the hardness in her eyes; they were eyes that had seen a lot. I was momentarily overwhelmed by a kaleidoscope of feelings that spun slowly through me; intrigue, curiosity, fear yet excitement too. Jessica seemed to have some purpose for me and I wasn't sure just what it was. I felt like I was in a movie but I had no script and didn't know what I was supposed to do next. I was tense and the air was stifling. Then she hugged me tightly, stood up and stretched luxuriously, like a big tigress waking from a nap.

"I didn't mean to scare you Judy. I read somewhere that everybody has a twin. Don't worry about it. I think it would be fun, though, if we told people we were sisters, don't you?"

I bit my lip, afraid to answer. I didn't want to hurt her feelings but I thought it was a strange idea, like something teenagers would do. She padded gracefully to the bathroom and returned with two thick white towels. Tossing me one, she winked. "Come on sweetie! Let's feed those boys and work on our tans. It's a beautiful day."

I stood up and followed Jessica to the pool, *telling myself the knot in my stomach was just hunger.*

Fun in the Sun with Jessica

essica and I talked on the phone frequently after our swim date. I was busy with work and my class and it was hard, with my chronic illness, to keep up with everything.

But after I turned down her lunch invitations several times in a row, she grew exasperated with my schedule and my excuses and her persistence confirmed my suspicion that she was lonely. I felt guilty for putting her off so much so I invited her and the boys to go to Art Fest, Scottsdale's annual arts and crafts festival. I knew it would be a stretch for me to spend a long day at the festival but I sucked it up and told myself I could do it. I knew the day afterwards I could rest and recuperate since I didn't have to work. Jessica enthusiastically accepted my invitation and I was glad I'd asked her, since I tended to be a hermit and sometimes had to force myself to get out of the house and socialize.

When I woke up Saturday morning it was already hot and humid out so I showered and slipped on a blue cotton sundress and braided my long, heavy hair. As Trevor and I pulled up to the Wilsons' home I noticed a shiny black Jaguar parked next to Jessica's silver BMW. Jessica answered the door wearing a tight-fitting tank top, white shorts and sandals. She looked calm and content and her skin glowed as if she'd had a facial. She ushered us in and Trevor went to the boys' room to find them. A tall, solidly built man with thick brown hair and wire-rimmed glasses walked into the living room, tucking a polo shirt into his pants. His hair was slightly disheveled, as if he'd just gotten out of bed. "Judy, this is my husband Nicholas," Jessica said.

I tried not to show my surprise. He smiled at me and shook my hand. His grip was firm and cool.

"Hi Judy. Jessica's told me all about you." He stepped back and shook his head. "I thought she was exaggerating but she's right . . . you do look a lot alike. Wow, that's weird!"

I blushed and smiled. "Yeah, we'll have to do a "family tree" and see if we connect somewhere back there in the Midwest!"

He nodded and looked at his watch. "I've got to get going. I'm late for an appointment." He pulled out his leather wallet and handed some money to Jessica. "Here honey. You can use it for Art Fest."

Jessica kissed him enthusiastically. "The admission price has gone up again this year. I enjoy going but everything is so expensive! A hot dog is $5.00!"

Nicholas sighed and frowned slightly and pulled out some more money. "Here's another $50. That's all I have with me. Will that do it?"

Jessica beamed and hugged him. "Yes, that will really help. Thanks Nicholas!" They embraced tightly and I felt embarrassed as they tongue locked. After a lengthy, passionate kiss, Nicholas pulled away.

"I'll be here to pick up the boys on Tuesday at 5:30. I'm taking them to a movie." He waved and headed towards the front door.

"That sounds great." Jessica followed him out to his car and they kissed again before he drove off. She came back in and draped herself languidly across her white leather sofa, then yawned and inspected her nails. "What'd you think of Nicholas? Pretty classy, huh?"

"Yes, he's very attractive. But I though you guys were getting a divorce. What happened?"

She shrugged her shoulders and winked at me. "Sex! That's what happened!"

I felt a bit flustered. "Well, I figured that out. I mean . . . . I thought you were through with him. I'm just surprised." "He came over last night to see the boys and one thing led to another and we ended up in bed."

"I see. So you guys are back together then?"

"Looks like it. He promised he'd stop seeing his little slut. We're going to dinner Friday."

"Oh, that's nice." I had anticipated her being sad and upset again today and, although I was happy for her, the sudden change in plans confused me. One day she was getting a divorce, the next she was in love again. I sat down on the sofa next to her.

"He'll probably buy me some fabulously expensive jewelry. He always does after we fight, especially after he's knocked me around."

"Jessica! He beats you?" I was horrified to think that the pleasant man I'd just met was a wife beater!

She shrugged her slim shoulders. "Yeah, he has before. He's even put me in the hospital a few times." She spoke casually, as if it were no big deal.

"Why do you take him back Jessica?"

"He's loaded Judy! He gives me the kind of lifestyle I deserve. And he'll inherit a ton of money when his father kicks off."

I was silent for a moment, trying to digest the information she had just given me. I couldn't relate to staying with a man just for money. And if someone hit me, he'd be history! My view of her seemed to change from moment to moment. It was the beginning of my disenchantment with Jessica.

She sat up and took my hand. "Judy, I hope I'm not scaring you away." Her voice was soft and soothing. "I really like you. Please don't think I'm a bad person. It's just that I've worked hard to be a good wife and I've tried to make peace with his family but they've never given me a chance."

I squeezed her hand. "Jessica, we all have our own paths to follow. I don't judge you." But as soon as the words were out of my mouth I wondered if I was lying. Because frankly, she WAS scaring me, or at the very least confusing the hell out of me. Yet I still felt kind of protective of her. "Is Nicholas moving back in?"

A shadow crossed her face. "Not yet. He thinks he should stay at his parents' house for now. But I'm sure he'll be back pretty soon. Anyway, I don't mind; this way I have the best of both worlds. A husband to support me financially but time to myself too." She stood up. "Speaking of time to myself, let's get going! I always enjoy the scenery at Art Fest. Lots of handsome men!"

"Hey, you just said you wanted to stay married," I teased her.

"Well there's no harm in looking, is there?" She replied with a grin.

"I guess not. And Jessica, I really do wish you well. I hope it works out with Nicholas." I tried to feel happy and positive for her but I was concerned. I knew just one night of sex didn't really solve problems like infidelity and abuse. But she seemed pretty confident so I told myself to mind my own business. And maybe they would be just fine. Maybe.

On the way to Phoenix, Camelback Road was crowded with cars heading towards Art Fest. The boys were in the back seat, horsing around with some action figures, lost in their own little world. Jessica asked me about my job and seemed impressed to learn I was the top salesperson at the publishing firm I worked for.

"Sometimes I miss the independence of making my own money. I was an excellent legal secretary, if I do say so myself. Hell, I know enough to outsmart most lawyers I know, including Nicholas!"

"Jessica, why don't you get your law degree? Then you really would be self-sufficient," I suggested.

She wrinkled her nose. "I'm too old!"

"You are not. Lots of people go back to school in their 40s."

"I guess the truth is, I don't want to work anymore. Nicholas has been hounding me to get a job but I refused. I figure, he married me, he can continue to provide me with the lifestyle I'm entitled to!"

"Well, if he has a lot of money like you said, why does it matter to him if you work?"

"I guess he wants to feel like he's in control of me. But he's not and never will be." She tossed her head and ran her fingers through her shimmery hair. I glanced at her out of the corner of my eye. I guess I was a little jealous. I had worked since I was 15 and the thought of not having to work for a while appealed to me. I suspected she was a bit spoiled and lazy. But I would never have said anything to her. I had a habit of watching people and thinking things about them but keeping the thoughts inside my head. I guess I was a kind of voyeur of life. I tried really hard not to judge anyone. This habit was good to a point but it sometimes left me stewing with confusing emotions. I was so afraid of hurting people or making them sad or angry, that I sometimes hurt MYSELF.

We were half-way across town when suddenly Jessica sat up straight and pointed out the window. "Turn right here!" She demanded.

Since we needed to go straight I didn't understand her request. "Why?"

"I need to stop at K-Mart. Turn, quick Judy!"

I felt annoyed and rattled. I didn't like people making changes all of a sudden when I had something planned. I sighed and reluctantly turned on my blinker so I could switch to the right lane. "Can't we stop later?

The traffic is so . . ."

"NO!" She yelled. "I need to go there now dammit!" Her voice was shrill and loud.

My jaw dropped and I felt like I'd been punched in the stomach. I had an urge to slap her in the face but at the same time, part of me felt like a child who had to bow to her demand.

My hands shook as I gripped the steering wheel and turned towards K-Mart.

"I'm sorry Judy." She quickly softened her tone. "I didn't mean to snap at you. I just really need to run in there. It will only take me two minutes."

I let out a breath and nodded. "Okay, that's fine. You just took me by surprise." I was still hurt but I told myself she didn't mean it. And she had apologized. We pulled into the parking lot of the store and I double-parked near the front.

"This is fine. Just stay here. I'll be right back." She quickly slid out and slammed the door.

I turned on the radio to my favorite "Oldies" station and leaned my head back while we waited. My thoughts were spinning with all that had happened already today and I was baffled by Jessica's mood changes. I closed my eyes and rubbed my aching head. After 10 minutes had passed, she still wasn't back and I began to get annoyed. Someone poked me in the back and I turned around. Jayson Wilson smiled tentatively at me and bit his lip.

"Excuse me Mrs. Kirkpatrick, but I need to go to the bathroom." He spoke softly, almost as if he were afraid.

"And we're dying of thirst Mom!" Trevor chimed in. I sighed and took some money out of my purse. I didn't have any ones so I gave Trevor a ten dollar bill and instructed him to buy each of them one drink only and nothing else, use the restroom and come right back. No sooner had they disappeared from my sight when Jessica came out another door, holding a plastic bag and drinking a bottle of water. She walked slowly, like she was balancing a tray on her head. She slid into the car, letting in a blast of hot air.

"Where are the boys?" She shrieked, as if they'd been kidnapped.
"They went to use the restroom and get sodas," I replied.

"You shouldn't have let them go! We've got to get a move on!" I shook my head. I was really getting bent out of shape and I had to force myself to breathe deeply. I wanted to explode at her. She opened her plastic bag and pulled out some lipstick and applied it while admiring herself in the mirror.

"Jessica, is that lipstick the reason we stopped?" I demanded. The nerve of her!

She gave no indication that she heard me and kept staring at herself in the mirror.

"God, look at those lines around my eyes. I look terrible. I'm going to need a facelift pretty soon. You're so lucky Judy. You don't have any wrinkles yet." She slammed the mirror shut and turned towards me. Her eyes narrowed as she peered at me. "But you need more color in your face. Here." She fished through her purse and pulled out an eyeliner pencil, reached over and touched my face gently. "Hold still!" she demanded. I sat stiffly while she carefully lined my eyes. Then she applied her new lipstick to my lips. Finally she pulled out a compact with a blusher and added color to my cheeks. "Voila! Check yourself out!" She shoved the mirror in front of me. I had to admit, I liked the way I looked. She hugged me and kissed me lightly on the cheek.

"Judy, you're so beautiful! Just relax. There's really no rush." Her voice was low, almost hypnotic. I felt myself start to relax. I sort of wanted to stay mad at her but I was just too exhausted. I wondered if I were the one at fault. Maybe I was too rigid. Jessica had her moods, for sure, but then, so did I. I made a decision to just let the rest of the day happen and stop worrying. Jessica smiled and took a bag of chocolate candy out of her bag and offered me some. It was tempting but I shook my head.

"Thanks but I can't eat sugar. Makes me hyper," I explained.

"Oh for God sakes, loosen up. Have a couple!" She shoved a piece of candy under my nose.

The smell of chocolate was so delicious I almost bit it out of her hand. Suddenly I recalled a movie I'd seen in which a man was offered a line of cocaine by someone. He had refused, saying "That's the Devil's candy. I bite into that and you own my soul." I shivered.

"NO Jessica!" It pissed me off that she didn't accept my explanation, that she kept pushing me. God she was wearing me out again. Finally the boys returned and they shoehorned themselves into the back seat, acting silly and happy. Trevor had spent most of my $10 on sodas and chips for them but I didn't say anything. I just wanted to get going. As I fastened my seatbelt and adjusted my mirror, Jessica touched my arm.

"Wait. I've got a surprise for you. You'll like this." She took an orange magic marker out of her K-Mart bag and, with a wicked gleam in her eye, put her arm out and proceeded to draw some kind of design on her wrist. "We can get in free at Art Fest! I have a friend who works there and he called me and told me how to sneak in! I do it every year! Saves money."

My stomach tightened. "But Jessica, Nicholas gave you plenty of money!"

"So? I can use that for something else. Maybe I'll get myself a massage or a facial next week. Come on, give me your wrist and I'll fix you up."

"Oh, no thanks," I said. My headache was getting worse and I felt shaky and angry.

"Listen, you don't have to be scared. Everybody does it." She reminded me of Trevor when he was trying to talk me into something I didn't want him to do.

"I'm not scared. I just don't feel right about it."

"Come on, don't be silly. I know you don't have money to blow. And neither do I. This will help us both out." She reached for my arm again and at the same time I pulled away from her.

Her eyes narrowed and she glared at me. "Oh, I see. You don't approve." Her tone was icy.

I felt sick. My Chronic Fatigue always kicked in when I was under stress. I started feeling nauseated and dizzy. I hated confrontations with people. I didn't consider myself a saint but I tried to operate my life with morals. I didn't want to set a bad example for Trevor. And why did I feel like I had to defend myself when she was the one who was wrong? This day was turning into a huge hassle. "You go ahead Jessica. I'm not doing it."

I held my breath, waiting for her to explode. For a brief moment, her face contorted into a grimace that was scary. Then she smiled as if nothing was wrong. "You know, you really are a good person. I knew you'd be a good influence on me." Or you'll be a bad one on me, I thought to myself! She turned towards the back seat. "Okay Wilson boys, give me your wrists." She marked her boys with the orange pen. I felt protective of them; they were innocent and they were being taught to cheat. Trevor looked at me with a solemn expression and raised eyebrows but didn't say anything. The air was stifling and I felt like I was going to faint. Gritting my teeth I started the car and headed out of the parking lot, wishing I'd stayed home, safe in my condo. Dealing with people often wore me out. I told myself to shake it off and try to have a good time but my patience was worn thin.

As we approached downtown Phoenix, there was an air of gaiety everywhere. A large section of streets had been blocked off with sawhorses and a tall barbed-wire fence circled the festival area. Crowds of people wearing loose-fitting summer clothing swarmed towards the gates. After driving around ten minutes to find a parking space, we finally found one in a gated lot and, to her credit, Jessica paid the $5.00 fee. I thought about asking her for the money I'd loaned her boys for sodas and chips but decided that would be petty, even though it had cut into my own funds. We all got out and headed towards the main entrance. At the gate, Jessica and her boys breezed in ahead of us after showing the man their wrists. I fleetingly thought of the $20 I could have saved if I'd joined in her scam.

We all stood in the middle of the fairway to get our bearings. There was a long row of refreshment stands off to one side. All kinds of food was being sold, including ethnic specialties like Greek pitas and Italian sausage. I inhaled the smell of buttered popcorn and pretzels; the aromas were delicious. There was another row of booths offering beer, soft drinks and lemonade.

Tanned people in swimming suits were splashing each other with hoses. One whole section of a field was full of children's rides. Jessica and I bought tickets for the boys to use on the rides.

"Let's give the kids an hour to themselves. Then we can have some fun on our own," Jessica suggested. I looked around. Most of the people looked harmless; parents and children mostly.

"I guess that would be okay." I always got nervous leaving Trevor out of my sight. We told the boys to stay together and take care of each other. Trevor was so excited he practically danced in place. "I got it Mom. Don't worry!" Jayson wore a watch so we told them to meet us back at the front gate in one hour. He flashed Jessica a fleeting smile as he walked away. He seemed like a sweet, sensitive child but there was a sadness around his eyes that bothered me. He led the other two boys towards the rides.

Jessica and I bought some lemonade and sauntered around, inspecting beautiful artwork in various booths. There were dozens of paintings of lighthouses in one area, while another booth sold tie-dyed shirts and dresses, reminding me of my "hippie" days. We stopped to inspect some turquoise and coral jewelry. Jessica had a sharp wit and at times reminded me of a comedian on Saturday Night Live. As we walked around she kept up a running banter like a ventriloquist's dummy, making fun of people. Soon I was laughing and the stress of earlier evaporated. As I watched her talk to some attorneys we ran into, I had the realization that I was a student of life and right now, Jessica was my new teacher. I had moved to Scottsdale from the Midwest five years previously. Although I had changed my style considerably since the transition, losing 10 pounds to fit in with the "you can never be too thin or too rich" mentality of Scottsdale, I still didn't feel like I belonged sometimes. It wasn't that I wanted to change myself drastically; I wasn't that shallow or vain.

But all of my life I had always sought to improve myself and when I watched the strong, successful women of Scottsdale, I longed to possess the aura of calm, indifferent poise they reeked of, like an expensive perfume that left a lingering scent of money and sexuality and power. I had a feeling Jessica could teach me these things. I listened to her and absorbed information like a sponge.

As we walked, we checked out the attractive guys that passed us and I had fun, feeling like I was a teenager again, out with a girlfriend. Jessica really strutted her stuff and she giggled to me that she had had her "boobs" done and that she was glad she didn't have to wear a bra anymore! I was used to getting my share of attention from men but, next to her in her sexy tank top, I felt like a dowdy brown sparrow. The rejection from Troy had really flat lined my self-esteem. As the men gawked at Jessica, we checked them out too. I tended to go for the guys with handsome faces, long hair and blue jeans. Jessica liked the men dressed in polo shirts and Rolex watches.

I noticed a cute guy with auburn hair pulled back in a ponytail and pointed him out. Jessica shook her head and sneered.

"Of all the guys here Judy! That's one of Nicholas's brothers!" She shook her head.

"Oh really? Great. Introduce us!" I said eagerly.

"Forget it sweetie! He's gay!"

"Darn! What a waste!" I laughed.

"Yeah. But besides that, I don't get along with him. Like I told you, Nicholas's whole family treats me like shit."

"God that must be really uncomfortable. What happened?"

"They're just snobby rich people. They think they are too good for me, since I wasn't raised with a silver spoon in my mouth. Nicholas's dad is the worst. He actually threatened to disinherit Nicholas if he married me!"

"Wow! That's nasty. Did he do it?"

"No. He's just a lot of hot air," she said dismissively. We bought some popcorn and stopped in front of a booth where a little person was sitting on a high stool making animal shapes out of colorful balloons for kids. There was a small crowd watching him. He had thick dark eyebrows like caterpillars and wore a silly brown beret; he looked like Humpty Dumpty. He noticed Jessica and he smiled in admiration.

"Hey Pretty Lady! What are you up to?"

Jessica's eyes narrowed. "About 5'9 shrimp!"

He winked at her. "Well I like tall women!"

Jessica muttered sarcastically under her breath, but loud enough for him to hear. "Yeah, I'll bet you're real popular with them."

He bristled with indignation and sat up straighter. "Hey, as a matter of fact I am! Don't knock it 'til you've tried it!"

Jessica smiled and sauntered up to him. "Maybe you're right, Small Stuff." She leaned in towards him, giving him a full view of her cleavage. His jaw dropped and he smiled broadly and reached out to hug her. She leaned in just a bit further, as if she were going to kiss him and in the process, she bumped into him and he fell crashing to the ground with a loud "thump".

"Oww! Dammit! You did that on purpose!" He rolled over and tried to stand but fell over again. Jessica was hunched over, holding her hand over her mouth, laughing hysterically. Several people nearby laughed too. I felt sorry for him but I had to fight hard to keep a straight face.

"It was an accident!" She was laughing so hard she had to wipe the tears from her eyes.

"The hell it was." He sputtered as he finally managed to stand up and brush himself off. "That was mean!"

"Well, maybe you should keep your mouth shut when you see a couple of ladies walk by!" Jessica retorted. Her playful mood had vanished; in fact she suddenly looked furious.

"Ladies! Well, maybe your friend is," he gestured to me, "but YOU sure aren't a lady. You're a bitch!" Jessica raised her arm to slap him but I grabbed it and pulled her away from him.

"You little Fucker!" She sputtered.

She allowed me to lead her away, shaking her head as we walked. "Judy, that wasn't my fault. That little asshole. I hate midgets. I've always hated midgets! They really annoy me."

I shook my head. Jessica had the strangest opinions, I thought to myself. Personally I felt sorry for people that were often the butt of jokes. I glanced at my watch, seeing it was almost time to meet the boys. Thank God. I'd had enough today of her behavior. She was exhausting me. Suddenly she stopped in her tracks. "Judy, this is so much fun. I have an idea. Let's take the boys home and come back later and have some real fun!"

"I'm tired Jessica. And I don't have a sitter for Trevor."

"That's no problem. They can all stay at my house. They have my cell number to call if they need me."

"I don't think so. I'm not ready to leave Trevor alone at night." To myself I wondered how she could leave her boys alone. They were way too young!

She frowned and crossed her arms. "Oh really Judy? That's not what I heard."

"What are you talking about?" I asked, indignant.

"Trevor told us you left him alone with the janitor!"

"What?!!"

"Yes Miss Perfect. He said a couple of weeks ago you went out of town and left him with the janitor!"

"I did no such thing!" I was incredulous. "That's ridiculous! I left him with Steve, a good friend of mine who happens to be a handyman. He fixed some things around the condo for me and stayed with Trevor." I shook my head, wondering what else Trevor had told people. A few weeks ago, I'd found out that he had been telling a neighbor that I didn't feed him, in order to get free food from her! I suddenly burst into laughter. Jessica began laughing too and we roared until tears ran down our faces. As we headed back to meet the boys, I had to admit to myself that her irreverence was part of my attraction to her. Jessica had become my new playmate.

CHAPTER FOUR

The Lady in White

For the next few months, I only saw Jessica occasionally, when I ran into her at school functions or in the grocery store. She and Nicholas were trying to patch their marriage up and I was busy finishing my screenplay for class. Then she called me one evening and said she had a surprise and asked if I could get off work early the next day and go with her to a "fabulous" event. Since I had vacation time coming, I agreed, curious to find out what she had planned for us. She told me to wear something elegant and to make sure it was black. I had to admit I had missed her a bit; things were never boring with Jessica. The fact that her unusual personality left me uncomfortable at times was something I pushed aside. I told myself that she was basically a good person, that she just had a bawdy sense of humor. And at the beginning, most of the time, I believed it.

The next morning I put on a two-piece black linen outfit and my favorite silver earrings. I had butterflies in my stomach as I dabbed on some "White Linen" perfume and carefully painted my nails a deep burgundy. I had a feeling the afternoon would be interesting. I went to work and left a couple of hours early and met Jessica at the fountain in front of my office building. I got into her shiny BMW and was surprised to see that she wore a white mini-dress with a matching jacket and white pumps "Jessica, why did you tell me to wear black if you're wearing white?" I was getting used to her quirks but I wanted to understand her and sometimes it was hard.

"It's part of the surprise Judy! You'll see! And you look awesome!" She was so smooth at brushing me off, you'd think I would resent her. But I didn't want to be petty so I just settled into my seat to relax. Jessica was especially vibrant and excited as she sang "Pretty Woman" along with the radio. Her mood was contagious and soon I was singing along with her as she dodged cars and trucks on the interstate. I felt happy that we were just out together for an afternoon, having a good time.

"When are you gonna tell me where we're going?" I asked as I touched up my lipstick using the mirror on the visor.

"When we get there!" She grinned. "You're as impatient as a little kid."

"So you and Nicholas are okay?" I asked casually.

Her eyes were covered with large sunglasses and I couldn't read her expression. "Actually the divorce is back on."

"Jessica! I'm sorry! I thought you had worked things out."

"Me too. But Nicholas wants the divorce. I don't care anymore."

Although she hid her pain, I knew she had to be devastated. I bit my lip and looked out the window.

"Hey, don't worry about me sweetie" she assured me. "I've got a great lawyer. I'm gonna make Nicholas sorry he ever crossed me." Her upbeat attitude surprised me.

"Well, good. I hope things work out for you."

"Oh, they will, believe me." She spoke with confidence and I decided to drop the subject.

She drove us to a part of town I had never seen before. I was enthralled by the breathtakingly beautiful homes. Jessica slowed down near a huge, stately brick church. There were cars lined up and down the streets near the church and around the block. Most of them were Rolls-Royces, Bentleys, BMWs and Jaguars, which were my favorite. Several long, black limousines were parked in front of the building. I was awestruck.

"We're going to a wedding, aren't we?" I sat up straighter and felt almost giddy with anticipation. I'd never been to a Scottsdale wedding but I'd read about them in the society pages. Maybe I'd see some famous people here.

Jessica impatiently honked her horn at an old woman who was having a hard time parking. She could hardly see over the steering wheel. She seemed to be contemplating how to get her car into the space.

Jessica honked her horn again, loudly. The lady got flustered and her head started wobbling. The hat teetered and fell off. Jessica laughed, then she zipped around the woman's car, expertly backed into the empty space at an angle and smoothly straightened her car out. The old lady leaned on her horn. Anger rushed through me; I had a soft spot for senior citizens, probably since I'd been so close to my grandparents. I hated seeing people taking advantage of them.

"Jessica that was cruel!" I protested.

She turned off the engine, threw her keys in her handbag and turned towards me, her green eyes narrowed into angry slits. "Grow up Judy! That wasn't "cruel"; that was nothing. Come on, we're late!" Her words were curt and I suddenly wished I had stayed home. I forced myself to take deep breaths. For a second I almost hated her; I was worn out again with her bratty behavior and disregard for other people and mad at myself for staying involved in her life.

She sighed and her expression softened. She put her hand on my cheek and turned my head towards her. "I'm sorry Judy."

I grudgingly allowed her to lift my chin; our eyes met. She cocked her head to the side and stroked my hair, like a mother would her child. "I'm not nearly as nice as you. I wish I were. I just do these things sometimes. That's why I need you around me. To keep me in line. Will you forgive me?"

I sighed and my muscles relaxed. Staying angry with people was hard for me and, although I knew that she was manipulating me again, I was caught in her mesmerizing spell. "I guess so. Just don't do it again."

She beamed and hugged me. "Let's go!" She gracefully got out of the car, straightened her shoulders and strutted towards the church. I had to admit, I admired her spunk. I got out and stepped up next to her and found myself imitating her classy strut. I shook off the incident in the car and breathed in fresh air. I was going to have a good time today! We made our way down the streets towards the church, past clusters of people who stopped talking and stared at us. I was puzzled by their reactions but Jessica had a bemused smile on her face and seemed not to notice the raised eyebrows and shocked expressions. I kept my poise until an attractive, middle-aged woman with red hair caught my eye and I realized she was glaring at us intently.

"What's her problem?" I whispered.

"That's Nicholas's aunt. She hates me. Just ignore her." Jessica replied in a stage whisper.

"Why is she here?"

"Shh. You'll find out."

As we got closer to the front door of the church it was increasingly obvious to me that we were being gawked at. I theorized it was because Jessica was so stunning in her white mini-dress and because of our resemblance to each other. As we passed a car window, I caught sight of our reflections and was reminded of matching queens on a chessboard, one dark and one white. It was a striking vision and I figured that the onlookers must think so too. I noticed that most of the other people wore black or other dark colors and their expressions were very serious. A queasy feeling inside me told me that something was not quite right here but I pushed it aside. I reminded myself that the very rich liked to wear black because it was elegant and classy, and they were probably stone-faced because it was chic to act blasé. We stepped inside the church, which had a high ceiling and rich oak pews with velvet padding. The room was packed with people, again most wearing black. Brilliant displays of flower arrangements graced the entire front of the church; even from a distance I could tell that they were all very expensive. When we first entered, there was a steady, low buzz of conversation but, as Jessica paraded up the aisle, an eerie hush fell over the room. She walked like a bride, taking one step, then another, as if they were all gathered there for her. I kept following her but I was so busy noticing the strange reaction of the crowd, I didn't realize at first that she had stopped and I almost ran into her. Then I froze.

Jessica stood in front of an open casket; in it lay a pasty-faced, quite elderly man whose mouth was turned down in a rigid frown. I tiptoed up and stood next to her and saw a wicked smile on her face. I was afraid to turn around; I could feel a hundred eyes boring a hole in my back. I felt like I'd been punched; I had never felt so conspicuous in my life.

"What the hell is going on?!" I hissed.

"A celebration Judy." She stared at the dead man intently, her eyes wide, almost as if she were in a trance. "A day I've been anticipating for a very long time."

"Who is he?" My whispered words sounded like rocks crashing against the walls of the deadly quiet room.

"My father-in-law. You want to talk about "cruel"? This man was cruel! I just found out he did cut Nicholas out of his will, so I couldn't touch any of his precious money. Son-of-a-bitch! He treated me like shit from the first day I met him." She giggled and there was a look of hysteria in her eyes. I realized she was living in crazy town at that moment. I scanned the room and spotted an exit off to the side, but before I could escape, Nicholas Wilson thundered towards us, his face mottled in anger. I stepped back, out of his way, leaving Jessica in the line of fire.

"You bitch! What the hell do you think you're doing?!" He was breathing heavily and sweating profusely. Gasps of horror and shock rippled through the room like a snake slithering across the grass.

Jessica stood her ground, glaring at him defiantly. "Why Nicholas, I've come to pay my respects darling!"

She reminded me of a she-wolf, baring her fangs, ready to attack.

"The hell you have! Get out of here!" He roughly grabbed her arm and tried to pull her towards the exit. She struggled wildly and managed to scratch his face with her fingernails.

"Ouch. God Dammit!" Nicholas winced in pain and gingerly touched his wounds. His nostrils flared and he grabbed her shoulders with both hands and shook her. She clutched his arms and pushed him. He bucked like a wild horse, pulling her off her feet.

"Stop it! You're hurting me!" She screamed. In spite of myself, I was intrigued. It was almost like they were engaged in foreplay, and even more fascinating, I had the feeling they were enjoying themselves!

"You're crazy!" Nicholas roared. Jessica twisted from side to side, gritting her teeth. The crowd began shouting as if they were at a wrestling match. Gone was the pretense of class and elegance; these people were getting down and dirty.

"Stick it to the bitch!" came a male voice.

"Kick him in the nuts honey!" yelled an elderly woman.

As the struggle went on, I just stood there, mesmerized like everyone else there. Suddenly I felt something sharp hit my back. I turned around and saw an elderly, hefty woman who was breathing hard and waving a black cane in the air.

"You're the bitch's long-lost sister. I heard about you!" She aimed her cane at my forehead. I put up my arms to ward off the blow. "The nerve of you two, showing up here!"

I grabbed the cane and wrenched it from her hands. "I am NOT her sister and you have no right to hit me!" With all the pent up frustration I'd been feeling about Jessica, it was all I could do to keep from smacking the woman across the face.

"Judy, help me!" Jessica wailed. I turned around and saw that she was hysterical now. Nicholas had her arm bent behind her back and was obviously hurting her. "He's going to kill me!"

I was beyond furious at her for bringing me here and starting this whole ruckus but I didn't want her to get hurt. I raised the cane and whopped Nicholas on the shoulder as hard as I could.

"Ouch!" Nicholas let go of Jessica and turned around to face me but then his eyes widened and he looked past me, over my shoulder. His expression turned to fear. "Mother!" He strode past me and I turned in time to see the elderly woman who had been hitting me, clutching her heart, her face a chalky white. She collapsed in a pool of black silk and taffeta, making a very loud thud on the floor.

"I can't breathe!' she gasped. Nicholas completely forgot Jessica as he hovered over his mother. At least a dozen men and women ran up to the front of the church yelling, "I'm a doctor!" They formed a tight circle around Mrs. Wilson and Nicholas like flies on a horse. I mentally said a prayer of thanks for my reprieve from Nicholas's wrath, then noticed Jessica standing a few feet away, seemingly very calm, like an actress who was taking a break from a scene she was rehearsing. I decided it was time for me to take control and I scooted over to her and took her arm.

"Let's go!" I commanded. Jessica seemed entranced by the scene taking place and she balked.

"Jessica, I'm leaving right now, with or without you. Come on!

Otherwise I'm going to let you fight your way out of here alone!" I felt a rush of energy as I gave her directions; for once, I felt like I had the upper hand instead of her bossing me around. She hesitated, then nodded. We scurried out the nearby exit and walked as fast as our heels would let us to her car. I knew this was a day I would never forget. By the time I got home I felt like I'd been in a sauna too long.

As I walked in the front door, I felt like a person arriving at Ellis Island, like I should be kissing the floor.

CHAPTER FIVE

Trouble

The next day I awoke from a fitful sleep with my head pounding. I called in sick to work, then called my AA buddy, Freddie, at his office. Freddie was a very successful real estate lawyer in Phoenix. We had dated a couple of years before and, although the romance had ended, we parted peacefully and stayed close friends. I had learned a lot from him and sometimes I still missed his calmness and sound advice. I had been so busy I hadn't talked to him in months.

"I heard about Mr. Wilson's funeral!" he said before I could even explain what had happened. I should have guessed; the Scottsdale grapevine was rapid and brutal.

"Freddie, it was a nightmare!"

"Judy, I had no idea you had been hanging around with her or I would have warned you. She's well known for her theatrics and has a terrible reputation in Scottsdale. You've got to stay away from her!"

"I know Freddie. God, it's so hard. I mean, sometimes I enjoy being with her but then she acts crazy and pulls these stunts. I feel kind of sorry for her. Nicholas's divorcing her and he beats her and he had an affair."

"Judy, you can't believe everything she tells you. She's notorious for fabricating things."

"Oh really?" I sighed. "Well I know there are two sides to everything . . ."

"Right; the truth and Jessica's version!" There was an edge to his voice which surprised me. Freddie was so laid back and rarely criticized anyone.

"Seriously?"

"Yes! I'm worried about you. You have such a big heart but you've got to be careful. You're too trusting."

I knew Freddie was right. I had a habit of taking broken people under my wings and trying to heal them. I was always rooting for the underdog and I had hurt myself, over and over, lending money to people, running their errands, listening to them for so long I got worn out. I had been in therapy for a couple of years, seeing a wonderful psychologist named Margie and she had helped me tremendously but I still had trouble with "boundaries".

"Judy, I know you. You'll probably keep seeing Jessica, won't you?" Freddie interrupted my thoughts.

"No! Absolutely not!"

"You promise?"

"I promise!"

"Well, I hope you mean that." He sighed. "She's nothing but trouble." Trouble. Yes, that was a good word for Jessica. Trouble with a capital 'T'. After talking to Freddie I felt better, stronger. I knew what I had to do; I had to let her go. I felt so much better that I got cleaned up and went into the office for the afternoon. I needed to stay on top of my job and I was not going to let Jessica interfere with my work or my sanity.

That night I was very tired when I got home from work. I had planned to call Jessica and explain that I couldn't go places with her anymore, that it was just too stressful for me. But my fatigue made my resolve fade and, for lack of courage and a better plan, I simply began screening my calls. Before I knew it, several days had gone by and I still hadn't "confronted" her. I just kept letting the machine collect her pleas for me to "pick up". Often I was tempted to answer; she sounded so forlorn and pathetic. I would turn the sound down but I could still hear the ring. I tried to ignore it but it began making me a bit crazy. I couldn't relax and read or do anything because the "ping" noise would interrupt me and I would scurry to the phone to see if it was her. I skipped church too because I knew I would probably run into her. That angered me, because I really liked the Scottsdale Community Church and wanted to keep going there. For some reason, I stopped answering calls from my other friends too. I felt like I was wrapped up in some kind of secret drama and I couldn't tell anyone. I even stopped answering

Freddie's calls because I was embarrassed to admit to him that I hadn't dealt with the "Jessica situation" yet. I had always tended to be a little overdramatic, maybe from reading too many Nancy Drew mystery books as a child. Anyway, I began turning my head away from neighbors when it looked like they were going to speak to me. This got a little tricky when I was riding in the elevator with one of my elderly neighbors.

One evening, Trevor and I were hanging out after dinner, enjoying ourselves. He was studying genetics in science class and was excited as he explained some of the things he had learned. He led me to the bathroom mirror and compared our eyes, noses, ears and fingers.

"Look Mom! I've got your ears! I think I got Dad's chin." He intently examined my fingers and then his own. It was a special moment and I didn't want it to end. I was flooded with love for him, so much that it hurt sometimes; my love was so fierce that it scared me. I decided I would bake his favorite chocolate-chip cookies. As he studied my toes while I got out the baking ingredients, the phone rang. I planned to ignore it but Trevor ran to answer it.

"Don't!" My voice was shrill and panicky; the strain of avoiding Jessica was getting to me.

"Mom!" He rolled his eyes. "What's your problem?" He grabbed the receiver. The happy bubble I'd felt around us popped and I felt my mood plummet to the floor.

"NO!!" I ran towards him and tripped over a stack of magazines, landing on my butt with my legs in the air. "Ouch!" I stood up slowly, gingerly rubbing my backside as Trevor answered the phone.

"Hello? Uh, well, let me see if she's around," he lied. Bless the kid. He did have a heart. He held the receiver to his chest and mouthed, "it's her." I shook my head "no".

Trevor spoke in a monotone. "I'm sorry Mrs. Wilson. She's sleeping. Can I take a message?"

A long pause. "Oh, really? That's too bad. Yes I know getting a divorce must be a drag. My mom got one too." Another pause. "He did? Bummer. Mrs. Wilson don't cry." He shook his head and gave me the finger. I cringed, feeling like a coward.

The next day was a Sunday. It was raining and Trevor was at a birthday party at the local roller skating rink. I decided I needed a break. Since watching movies was therapeutic for me, I had quite a collection of them. I had them alphabetically organized by title so I started with "A" and spent fifteen minutes trying to decide what to watch. I ended up putting "Gone with the Wind" in the VCR. It had been one of my favorite films when I was younger, but, as I watched it again, I realized that I disliked Scarlett O'Hara. She was so selfish and I hated the way she used people. I wondered how I could have thought she was so wonderful. Sure she was beautiful and charming but Rhett Butler would have done better to stay with Belle, the busty, flame-haired madam of the whorehouse! At least Belle was honest and had a heart, and she truly loved Rhett.

As I watched Scarlett eating lunch at a picnic with dozens of young men hovering around her, it dawned on me that Jessica reminded me a lot of Scarlett; superficial and heartless. Irritated that I hadn't picked something else, that I was AGAIN thinking about Jessica Wilson, I ejected the first half of the film and put the second half in. At least I could look at Clark Gable; that was time well spent since he had always been one of my favorite leading men. I fast-forwarded it to the end so I could get to the part I liked, when Rhett finally had enough of Scarlett.

A loud knock on my door interrupted my mental inventory of Scarlett's faults and I hit the "pause" button. Reluctantly I tiptoed over and squinted through the peephole. My heart pounded and I jumped back, shivering. Jesus! What the hell was that?! I quickly dead-bolted the door and cautiously re-examined the apparition outside. At first glance, it looked like a crumpled up mask from a costume shop, or perhaps some child's art project gone wrong. But, upon closer inspection, I realized that it was Jessica's face, grotesquely distorted, pressed against the peephole. Her nose was quite swollen and red blotches, like chicken-pox rashes, covered her skin. Her mouth was drawn and puckered as if she were sucking on lemons. As I hesitated, something white draped over her nose and I heard a loud "honking" noise as she blew it, much too thoroughly. I hugged myself as if to ward off the cold and chewed my lower lip, trying to figure out how to get rid of her. A catty little thought, like a footnote, meandered through my brain and lodged itself in my "Jessica" file; for the first time since I'd met her, she actually looked unattractive. No, that was being polite; she looked homely! So she wasn't flawless after all. Quickly, however, a wave of guilt washed over me and I chided myself for my meanness. What was the matter with me?

"Judy, please answer the door! I know you're in there!" She wailed and continued to pound. I stood there, trying to identify the emotions going through me. Suddenly I realized I was just plain pissed off. I shouldn't have to be ambushed like this. I lived in a gated community for a good reason, the assurance that I would not have unwanted guests. What the hell was going on here? I'd have to straighten those security guards out tomorrow. Finally I just accepted the fact that I was going to have to answer the door. Wanda, my chubby, nosy neighbor would be here soon to complain about the noise if I didn't. Shivering, I unlocked the dead-bolt, swung open the door and backed against the wall so I wouldn't get knocked over.

Jessica spilled inside like a woman's purse being emptied. Little wads of Kleenex sprayed out of her hands like balls from a child's popgun. She glared at me, fuming with anger, and her witchy face scared me. I stepped back. I was, once again, on the receiving end of her wrath. For a moment her eyes bored holes in me and she clenched her fists. She whooshed past me, leaving a trail of heady perfume and red-hot energy in her wake, then began pacing back and forth.

"Why haven't you answered my calls?" she demanded.

"I've been really sick." I dug my fingernails into the sweaty palms of my hands.

"Yeah, right. Don't lie to me. I drove by your office and saw your car parked outside."

I stepped back another foot. So she was stalking me now? "I'm sorry. I really haven't felt well. I had to force myself to go to work. I told you I have Chronic Fatigue Jessica. Sometimes I don't have the energy to talk."

"Judy, you're my best friend! How could you shut me out like that? You could have just told me you weren't feeling well. But to completely ignore me!" I could see past the anger as she stared at me. She reminded me again of that lonely, lost child. And saying I was her "best friend"? God, that was sad, even pathetic and also quite frightening. It was like having my toes in hardening cement. Was it too late to get out? The air was so full of tension, I felt like a piece of china about to break into a million jagged shards. I stepped toward her, slowly, cautiously.

"I'm sorry I haven't answered your calls Jessica. But that day, at the funeral . . . it was just too much for me. I don't think it was fair of you to drag me there and not even tell me what was going on."

She nodded and sighed deeply. Much of the anger left her face; now she just looked sad. "You're right. Sometimes I don't think things through. I'm so sorry Judy. I've been mad at Nicholas's family for so long. I just wanted to get back at them."

"I know you're been going through a rough time Jessica. I've been trying to help you. But that day was awful. I'm not like you. I don't like making scenes. I just want to live a quiet life."

Her shoulders slumped and she began to sob. "Oh Judy. I'm such a burden on you. I'm so sorry." Here it was; the moment of truth. I should agree with her, tell her that yes, she was like Mount Everest on my skinny shoulders. I should tell her to get a life, go home and do her dishes, get a damn job! And most of all, leave me alone! But, deep inside me, I had this strange awareness that Jessica had somehow managed to finagle me to hop on a 747 with her. I had no idea where we were going but I didn't know how the hell to get off and I didn't have it in me to shut the door on her. I was a sucker for a lost cause.

"You're not a burden Jessica." The lie just came out of my mouth like I had no control over it. Words that betrayed ME, words that kept me in a mire of my own making. "I'm still your friend."

"I don't know how you can stand me."

Just then, the movie came blaring back on, startling me. I felt irritable and shaky and I grabbed the remote from a nearby table.

"I can't stand myself sometimes!" Jessica went on.

"Frankly my dear, I don't give a damn!" Rhett Butler's voice loudly responded to Jessica's confession. I had to bite the insides of my cheeks to keep from laughing hysterically. I quickly turned Rhett off. Jessica continued talking and seemed lost in the ozone, as if she was unaware of anything but her own ramblings.

"I just felt like you were abandoning me, like Nicholas did, like my parents did, like everyone else in my life has. People are always leaving me. I should be used to it by now. Am I that horrible?"

She looked exhausted, like a very old woman. All my anger and fear of her vanished and I felt a rush of sympathy for her in spite of myself.

"No. You're a beautiful, strong woman." I walked towards her as if I were approaching a sick person in a hospital bed. I hugged her and she felt thin and fragile, as if, underneath her expensive feathers, she was a tiny bird, shivering from the cold.

"I love you Judy," she said softly. "I've never met anyone like you." She put her head on my shoulder and hugged me back. As we embraced, my tension melted and her tears subsided. I felt like we had become one person; it was hard to tell where her skin ended and mine began.

CHAPTER SIX

The Mission

While I was swimming laps on my lunch hour one day, the cold water stimulated me and my endorphins kicked in. I had one of those "ah-ha!" moments when I felt brilliant and creative, totally at one with the Universe. I had been reading a book about reincarnation, something I was trying to understand. It talked about how we should befriend people with "different vibrations" than ourselves and try to work things out with them, not always just be around people that were "easy" and comfortable. It said that the challenges that arose from being intimate with difficult, troubled people were learning experiences. And it dawned on me that Jessica had been put into my life for a reason; we could learn from each other. Just because Jessica was "trouble" didn't mean I should give up on her. As I floated on my back at the end of my swim, the sun warmed my face and I felt excited; in fact, I was almost burning with passion. I wondered if this was how Mother Theresa felt when she ministered to the poor. I had a plan, a mission; I finally knew what to do with Jessica Wilson.

Friday night at 7:30, Jessica and I rode in my car down Camelback Road. The musky scent of her perfume assailed my nostrils as I maneuvered through the heavy traffic. We were in the middle of "The Season", when thousands of tourists descended on Arizona and the wealthy residents came back from their summer homes to spend the winter in their mansions. I was dressed in blue jeans and a white shirt but Jessica wore a luscious mulberry two-piece outfit she had just bought from one of the shops in the more elegant areas of Scottsdale. I had a stab of jealousy as I glanced at her attire; I wished I could afford clothes like that. I had told her that I had a surprise for HER this time and she kept asking me where we were going. All I would reveal was that I was taking her to a place where she could find peace and serenity, and meet some really nice people. I had a knot in my stomach as I drove down a lane past cactus plants which lead to a secluded and cozy log house. I really hoped this wasn't a mistake. Some of my resolve had faded but I told myself to think positive. After all, how bad could it be? A rock garden and some picnic tables were nearby and people sat, talking and laughing. A large parking lot across from the house was filling up with cars and a motorcycle backfired as it slowly cruised to a halt. Dozens of people were streaming across the lot towards the building.

"What is this place?" Jessica asked as she peered out the window. "Some kind of a church?"

I pulled into an empty space and turned off the ignition. "Actually Jessica, this is the Cactus Club. I'm taking you to an AA meeting."

"AA? Why? I'm not an alcoholic Judy!" She gasped in horror.

"I know. This is an open meeting. You don't have to be an alcoholic to attend. I'm hoping it might help you feel better, calmer maybe."

"How do you even know about this place? Are you an alcoholic? I've never seen you drink."

"I'm a recovering alcoholic, yes. I haven't had a drink or a drug for about 6 years."

"Well that's great for you Judy. But you can't expect me to go in there! What if I see someone I know? This could be embarrassing!" She frowned and crossed her arms.

"Oh really? How much more embarrassing could it be than that hissy fit you threw at Mr. Wilson's funeral?!"

"Well . . . I said I was sorry about that . . ."

"This is an anonymous program Jessica. People who come here are asked not to tell anyone who they see here. That's the whole idea. It's just people, helping each other, supporting each other."

"Judy, you're sweet to be concerned about me but I don't need help."

"Wasn't that you at my house last week crying and telling me how miserable you were?"

"Well, yes, that's true . . ."

I sighed deeply. "Listen, why not just check it out? It's only one hour. You never have to come back again if you don't want to."

Her eyes filled with tears and she spoke softly. "You're right. I do need help. I'll come in with you."

I squeezed her hand. "It'll be okay." She followed me to the back porch of the house, where clusters of people sat at plastic tables, smoking and drinking coffee. The smoke made me nauseous and I hurried inside, glad they didn't allow smoking in the meetings anymore. In the kitchen there was a snack bar and I bought each of us a diet soda. As I sipped the cold drink, a radio played "Jody Girl", one of my favorite old Bob Seger tunes. It took me back to my early 20s and I felt a stab of sadness, remembered the great times I'd had, when my life was carefree. I greeted friends who were milling around, buying coffee, soft drinks or candy. Janet, a big-boned blond in her 40s who wore heavy makeup came over and hugged me.

"Judy! It's good to see you. I've missed you!"

"It's good to see you too Janet." I smiled. She was one of my best AA friends. She had been through a lot but never felt sorry for herself. She looked at Jessica and I with open curiosity.

"This has got to be your sister!"

I shook my head. "No, this is my friend Jessica. Tonight's her first meeting."

"Welcome!" Janet smiled warmly and hugged Jessica. "I still can't believe how much you two look like each other." Janet was a legal secretary and she and Jessica chatted, comparing notes about various law firms and attorneys in the area. When Janet gave Jessica her phone number, I was glad; I really wanted Jessica to make new friends. Although I had never seen her get drunk she behaved like someone on a "dry drunk", a term I had learned in AA for someone who is negative and unhappy most of the time. I hoped that the meeting might steer Jessica into a more enlightened mindset.

Several more of my friends came over and hugged me and I introduced them to Jessica. They hugged her and she seemed pleased, like a child who wasn't used to affection but longed for it. I was feeling better about bringing her here. Then Tommy, a tall, thin man wearing glasses held together with masking tape came over to give me a hug. I had a soft spot for him; he was homeless and "lived" at the Cactus Club, sleeping on a sofa in the recreation room and using the shower. He wore clothes from the thrift store and was missing several teeth in the front. He held out his hand to Jessica but she just frowned and looked him up and down with distaste. Her reaction didn't surprise me but it bothered me. Tommy was a sweetheart, always looking out for others and he was very sensitive. I could see the hurt expression in his eyes.

I led Jessica into the main room, which was full of chairs all facing towards a table at the front of the room. I wanted to sit in the front row but Jessica shyly asked if we could set towards the back which we did. It seemed her "scared little girl" side had come out again and I had a surge of tenderness for her. My mother had always taught me that we can "plant seeds" in people, introduce them to new experiences and ideas, but that we can't expect too much right away. Still, I prayed that Jessica would have a spiritual awakening tonight.

By 8:00 p.m. there were about 75 people there; all the seats were filled and many stood at the back of the room or sat on window ledges. Teenagers with pierced noses and chains hanging from their faded jeans mingled with 30-year-olds dressed in professional attire. White-haired, elderly folks sat together chatting. Most of them were smiling. I always got a buzz from the energy in the meetings and the way everybody was welcomed without judgment or bias. I glanced at Jessica and she was looking around the room, observing with curiosity. Two men sat at the table in front. Raymond, a man in his 70s who was leading the meeting, reminded me of Santa Claus with his white beard and rosy cheeks. He pounded a wooden gavel on the table and the conversation died down. He opened the meeting with "The Serenity Prayer". As we prayed out loud the cacophony of soft voices soothed me and I breathed a deep sigh; the prayer always made me feel calm and centered. Jessica bowed her head politely and listened. Raymond asked if there were any visitors or newcomers and a few people introduced themselves. I nudged Jessica and raised my eyebrows but she shook her head. I understood her shyness; I had felt that way too at my first meeting.

After someone read "The 12 Steps", Raymond lit several big white candles and the lights were turned off. The room took on an almost unearthly and peaceful glow. I felt like I was on a pink cloud. Raymond turned the meeting over to Chuck, a man in his 30s wearing wire-rimmed glasses and a shirt and tie. He told a fairly typical "AA Story", about how he started drinking as a teenager, got into lots of trouble, crashed cars and was in and out of jail. He straightened himself out for a while and got married, then his drinking escalated again and he almost lost his job and his wife. The good news was he went to rehab, then came to AA and had been clean and sober for two years now. His marriage was solid, he had a new baby boy, had a good job as an accountant and had just been promoted at work. I listened with interest; I always liked hearing how people had changed their lives for the better, by accepting spirituality. I believed people could change if they really wanted to. I was hoping that Jessica would come to realize that trying to get revenge and using people for financial gain and status was not the answer to her unhappiness.

Chuck opened the meeting for sharing and my favorite topic, "Gratitude" was chosen. Mary, a woman in her 50s with salt-and-pepper hair and a thick Boston accent talked about how, before she had found AA and God, she had always felt sorry for herself, felt like she was a "victim". I related to her story a lot and I was also hoping Jessica was absorbing this because she was, in my opinion, the classic "victim" all the time. Mary went on to say that she used to feel like her glass was "half-empty" all the time but she had changed her attitude and now saw it as "half-full."

Then somebody brought up "resentments" and it was discussed how we only hurt ourselves when we resented people. Jessica nodded her head. I was pleased; if she only got this part of the meeting I would feel like I'd accomplished something by bringing her here. At the end of the meeting a basket was passed. I put a dollar in and told Jessica that since she was new, she didn't have to contribute. She nodded and thanked me, whispering that Nicholas hadn't paid her the child support and alimony this month. I wondered if she was telling me the truth, thinking of the new outfit she wore. But I shrugged off my suspicions; it didn't matter to me. I wasn't perfect. I had my own life to worry about. As we all stood in a circle and held hands and said "The Lord's Prayer" I felt lighthearted and exhilarated.

When Jessica and I walked out to my car, her eyes were wide and she looked ready to cry. I figured she was just overcome with emotion, like me. I wondered if I was really witnessing Jessica having a psychic change. Goosebumps tickled my arms.

I looked her in the eye. "Thanks for coming in with me. How do you feel?"

She looked around the parking lot at everyone getting into their cars and shook her head. "I hardly know what to say!"

I held my breath; here it came, the moment I had been working for, waiting for, when the real Jessica Wilson would emerge, the butterfly I had glimpsed inside its' cocoon would spread its wings and fly. "Yes, I know what you mean."

She wrinkled her nose and shuddered. "I feel so sorry for you! God, I thought MY life was bad. You have to come to this dump and be around these losers! You poor thing!"

I watched her beautiful, perfectly shaped mouth move as she uttered those rotten words and I wondered how such a gorgeous creature could be filled with such ugly, toxic crap! So much for expectations. I was definitely ready to turn in my nuns' habit; my pink cloud was raining rotten tomatoes! I had to bite my tongue to keep from lashing out at her and clench my fist to keep from slapping her!

CHAPTER SEVEN

Jessica and her Boy - Toy

A few weeks later, Divine Intervention brought me a reprieve from Jessica. She called me one day, giddy with happiness. "Judy, I've met the most gorgeous man!" I listened as she raved about Josh Swenson, her new "squeeze". Josh was an attorney, ten years younger than her, whom she had met at a social function. He was, according to Jessica, "a total dream". Although I was still rather hurt by the way she had ripped my AA meeting and friends to shred, I was glad she had met someone. I was also very relieved, since I suspected this Josh would probably keep her busy. For the next few months, she was in a whirlwind courtship with him and I rarely saw or heard from her. When she did call, she was very happy. During that time period, my love life was basically non-existent and it was hard to keep hearing about hers but I truly wished her well.

In October, Jessica called and invited me to a Halloween party at her house and said she wanted me to meet Josh. She also promised that there would be a lot of single, attractive men there. Since I was rather lonely and bored, I decided to go. Besides, I was curious about meeting Josh.

The night before the party, Jessica and I took the boys to "Fright Night", an event held for the kids at the Community Center. We arrived as darkness fell and an orange harvest moon hung in the sky. As I got out of Jessica's car, I looked around at the scarce plants and shrubs and wished for a moment I was back in the Midwest, inhaling the smell of burning leaves and seeing their beautiful colors of burnt orange, brown, and shades of red. The boys had all eaten candy at Halloween parties at school and were wired on sugar and excitement. I was glad to see the Wilson boys having fun as I tended to worry about them. I knew Jessica loved them and tried to be a good mother but sometimes I felt her drama-queen antics and her selfishness confused and hurt the boys. In spite of everything they had gone through, they seemed to be sweethearts and I was touched when I saw Jayson, dressed as "Batman" hug his tow-headed little brother, who was his sidekick "Robin". Trevor wore a brown felt hat and carried a whip to emulate "Indiana Jones" his current hero. A "Haunted Forest" had been set up in a field next to the building and dozens of kids were in line with their parents. A dark tunnel had been created by draping black sheets over trees.

Ghosts, goblins, witches and all sorts of spooky creatures lurked in crevices and corners along the dark path behind broomsticks and bales of hay; spiders clung to cobwebs above us. We had to stand in line a long time and it was noisy; small children whined and some of the older ones had boom boxes playing obnoxious "thumping" music. I got tired and irritable but Jessica was floating on her "Josh high" and was unusually patient. As the boys kidded around, Jessica gushed to me about how wonderful Josh was, how great a lover he was, how much the kids liked him, the gifts he bought her, and every detail of their relationship down to the brand of underwear he wore! Her only complaint was that he "wasn't loaded with money" yet, due to his youth, and she saw that as a drawback, but she had no intention of letting him go. She vibrated with giddiness that bordered on obsession; she didn't even complain about Nicholas for a change. She confessed that she hardly ate or slept because she was so in love; she had never felt this way before and she was sure she had met her soulmate.

The following day as I pulled up in front of Scottsdale Prep School to pick Trevor up, I saw the Wilson boys getting into Jessica's car and I waved at them. Later, I took Trevor trick-or-treating, then picked up Jennifer, his favorite sitter, to stay while I went to Jessica's party. I had borrowed a "French Maid" outfit from my neighbor, Candy. It basically consisted of a little white apron, a tiny white headband and a black leotard. With it I wore black silk hose, black high-heels and a velvet choker. I combed my hair into a topknot and put on more make-up than I usually wore. I felt pretty sexy but also a bit uncomfortable. The shoes hurt my feet and I didn't really like to wear clothes that screamed "look at me", which was one of the big differences between Jessica and I. Plus, I frankly didn't like holidays; I guess I was a bit of a "Scrooge" but holidays just seemed to be a lot of frenzy and pressure and put expectations on people that were too high and usually ended up being disappointing.

I sighed and grabbed my purse. When I left some money with Jennifer for a pizza, I thought about just staying home and watching TV but instead I threw a jacket over my shoulders and kissed Trevor goodbye. It was chilly outside which pleased me immensely. I waved at one of my elderly neighbor couples dressed in cowboy and cowgirl outfits and shook my head as I watched them drunkenly teeter into the building.

Jessica's driveway was packed with expensive cars and each window in the front of her house had a candlelit jack-o-lantern in it. I parked down the street and even from a half block away I could hear "Disco Inferno" blaring from her house. I hated disco music and had to force myself to keep going but I promised myself that I wouldn't stay long. Roberta, Jessica's cleaning lady, opened the door, wearing a Gypsy Fortune-Teller costume. She was somewhere on the cusp between curvaceous and fat, an Hispanic woman in her 40s with her thick, frizzy black hair braided and wrapped like a wreath around her head. Her long, heavy dress was spangled and exotic, colorful as a peacock's plumage. I was surprised to see her but she told me that Jessica had hired her for the night to help out with the party. She was very gracious and led me to the spacious living room where dozens of "party animals" were drinking and dancing to "Macho Man". I smiled as I checked out the costumes; skeletons, devils, witches, a ballerina, a belly dancer, a "Richard Nixon", even a couple of "M&M"s! As "The Hulk" danced with a mummy in front of me, I recalled Jessica's promise of attractive single men and wondered with amusement how I was supposed to even tell the men from the women! For all I knew, there could have been a serial killer behind one of those masks. Roberta took my jacket to another room, then came out and led me to the kitchen. She thoughtfully remembered that I didn't drink and fixed me a glass of diet soda and a paper plate with some snacks on it.

"How are you feeling tonight?" Her Spanish was sensual and husky. "You are tired, no?"

"I'm okay . . . yeah a little tired. Thanks for asking."

"Sit down, please." She pulled out a chair and I gratefully sat. Then she slowly settled into chair across from me as if she were about to hatch an egg. Bemused, I noticed what beautiful cheekbones she had; she really was an attractive woman.

"Judy, may I tell your fortune?" I remembered Jessica telling me that Roberta had a little side business, as a psychic! I was intrigued; I'd had quite a few psychic experiences in my life.

Sometimes I had prophetic dreams. One night, years previously, I had dreamed that my grandmother was dying. My legs ached terribly during the night which was strange because Grandma had diabetes and had had a leg amputated. When I woke up the next morning, my pillow was soaked from my tears. A few hours later my dad called to tell me that Grandma had died during the night. Visions like this had happened to me quite often although I rarely told anyone; most people I tried to tell insinuated that I had fabricated the story. But I was very open to believing in the "unseen".

"Sure. Why not?" I agreed as I bit into a chunk of cheese on a cracker.

She pulled out a deck of Tarot cards from her skirt pocket. The cards were black on one side, twice the size of regular playing cards. She shuffled them and laid them in front of me to cut.

Then she spread them out on the table. I was intrigued by their strange-looking symbols and characters, suns and moons, knights and dragons. They were amazing but a little creepy. The center card had a knight holding a sword high over his head. Roberta's brows furrowed in concern. "Much conflict is coming into your life. You must be very cautious as events unfold. You must protect yourself and your child."

I held my breath. "My child? Trevor and I are in danger?"

She nodded. "You are too close to a perilous situation." She frowned at a card showing a black-hooded skeleton holding a scythe over his head. "This is the card of death!" she said throatily. "The bridge over which we all must go!"

My heart was hammering. "What are you saying?"

"Someone you know will die soon!" She said ominously.

I was starting to feel queasy, as if I were seasick. I was regretting the whole tarot card idea.

"Who? My son? Someone in my family?"

She shook her head. "No, not someone related to you. But someone you are connected with in many ways. There will be anger and betrayal and much pain."

"But what danger?" I persisted. "Is there anything I can do to prevent it from happening?"

"No. The events are already in motion. You cannot change them." Her eyes widened in fear and she froze as she stared over my shoulder. The hairs on the back of my neck stood up as a shadow passed over the room. "Elvira, the Goddess of Darkness" charged into the room with the crackling speed of a lariat and I felt an icy cold breeze across my bare shoulders. She descended upon us like a phantom, her floor length black dress rustling against the floor like mice.

"Roberta! What the hell are you doing?" Jessica's voice was hard and full of venom as she towered over us, sneering angrily. Her eyes were heavily lined with black and her costume was tight-fitting; as she glared at Roberta, I shuddered. "You're supposed to be working for me tonight!" Her voice was harsh and shrill and she was breathing so hard I thought she might faint. "I'm not paying you to sit around on your fat ass!"

"How dare you speak to me that way!" Roberta said indignantly.

"I can speak to you any way I want! You're my employee. You're . . ."

"Jesus Christ, calm down Jessica! ´" A deep male voice came from the doorway and I turned around to see none other than "Count Dracula" himself! He was about 6'2" and a black silk cape draped his broad shoulders. Even wearing "fangs" and frowning, he was extremely handsome and I knew right away it had to be Josh. His thick, sandy-blond hair was combed back with gel, revealing a wide, attractive forehead with a deep widow's peak. His eyes were piercing blue-green and his face was smooth shaven and tanned.

Jessica smiled through a scowl, her voice icy. "Josh, why are you always defending her?"

"Because I think you're out of line."

"Josh I don't need you to tell me how to handle the hired help!" Her eyes were pools of black fury.

"Hired help? God, listen to yourself! You sound like a slave owner!"

For a moment Jessica's face was so contorted in rage it looked like a hideous mask. Then she quickly rearranged her expression into a blank slate. It was like watching an actor changing roles in the middle of a performance. "Sorry, I guess I overreacted honey." She was full of sweetness now and Josh shook his head and sighed deeply, then walked over to her and put his arms around her. She melted and wrapped her silky strands of touch around him. There was a large mirror on the wall next to them and as they hugged, I could see Josh wink at Roberta behind Jessica's back and then his eyes swept me up and down appreciatively. I watched Jessica's face as she studied their reflections and as she observed his flirtation, her eyes narrowed and the veil of anger came over her again. But when she pulled away from him and turned to Roberta, she was as calm and emotionless as a newscaster talking about the stock market.

"Roberta, get back to work. Check and see if anyone needs a drink." Roberta nodded, her face impassive. She gracefully gathered her cards and, with the dignity of a queen, left the room.

I was very uncomfortable with the whole scene and wished I hadn't come; it was as if I'd just seen Cinderella berated by her Evil Stepmother. I felt sorry for Roberta; I sure wouldn't want to work for Jessica. I also thought Jessica was behaving stupidly; if I were Josh, I'd be totally turned off by her behavior. Jessica turned towards me. "Sorry Judy . . . she's just so lazy sometimes. By the way, you look fantastic! I love your costume!" She leaned in and hugged me and I reluctantly hugged her back. Then she smiled warmly at Josh as if nothing had happened.

"Honey, this is my friend Judy, the one I've been telling you about."

"Charmed!" Josh took my hand and kissed it after bowing over. "You make a beautiful maid! Are you for hire?"

I laughed nervously as I saw Jessica's eyes flash with jealousy. Josh commented on our likeness to each other and for once that seemed to bother her. She smiled tightly and said, "Yes, everyone says that."

"The Monster Mash" was playing from the other room and Josh asked me to dance. I accepted and followed his swirling cape to the living room, through the swaying couples, to find a place to dance. Josh was a good dancer and I had fun doing "The Twist" with him, but before the song was even over, Jessica appeared and watched him like a bloodhound after a rabbit. When she cut in on us, she bumped against me and I almost lost my balance. I backed away and headed down the hall to the restroom. I passed Roberta in the hall.

"Judy, one more thing. You must beware of a dark-haired women . . . she is evil!" Then she winked at me and smiled. I nodded, wondering if she really knew just how right she was.

When I returned to the living room, Jessica and Josh were in a corner making out, ignoring everyone else. Some of the guests were getting really drunk. Since I had quit drinking years ago, I didn't enjoy being around drunk people; it wasn't that I was jealous or wanted to join them. It was simply boring and annoying, listening to them repeat themselves. And, since I was always sober, I felt responsible for them when they tried to drive. I felt like I was their caretaker, an unwilling "designated driver" of life. It was getting louder and louder and I decided it was time for me to leave. As I slipped into my jacket, Jessica turned off the music and announced that the party was moving to the Safari Club, a popular nightclub in Scottsdale. I glanced at my watch.

It was only 10:00, still early, so I decided to join them and see if my night improved. On the way out, Jessica stopped me and handed me a shopping bag full of clothes, telling me she had cleaned out her closet and thought I'd like the outfits. I looked inside and found some nice black jeans, a black sweater and a couple of bathing suits, all good quality. I thanked her and left and drove to the Safari Club.

The nightclub was decorated like an African jungle; cacti bushes surrounded the dance floor and stuffed tigers and giraffes watched the crowd. It was wild; almost everyone was wearing a costume. Jessica and Josh danced hip to hip, ignoring everyone else, lost in their own little world. One of my favorite songs, "You're So Vain" by Carly Simon came to my mind as I watched them. They were acting like the King and Queen of Hell in their dark clothing and sneering faces. As I danced to "At The YMCA" by the Village People with Mike, a guy who worked in my office, I tried to loosen up but felt tired and depressed. At about 11:00 I left, feeling spent.

When I finally got home, Jennifer was watching TV. I paid her and she left, meeting her dad downstairs in front of my building. I tiptoed into Trevor's room and watched him sleep for a few minutes, trying to decompress from my evening. After I kissed him, I walked back into the living room, sat down and closed my eyes, grateful to be home. So much for my big evening out.

CHAPTER EIGHT

A Woman Scorned

I didn't hear from Jessica for a couple of months and I assumed things were still hot with Josh. Then one night, Jayson Wilson called me, crying and breathless. After I talked with him for a few minutes, trying to calm him down, he told me that Josh had broken up with Jessica and she was hysterical and was threatening to kill herself! Jayson pleaded with me to come over and help her. I dreaded getting mixed up with her again but Jayson said he couldn't reach Nicholas and didn't know what to do. I was very concerned about the boys so I reluctantly told Trevor to come with me and we drove to the Wilson house a half hour later.

As we walked up to the door, we could hear Jessica screaming like a fishwife. "God Dammit, you boys are driving me crazy! Shut that damn TV off and go to your room!"

Anger rushed through me. Trevor grabbed my arm. "Mom, maybe we should just go home."

"We have to help them honey. Those boys don't deserve this." The door wasn't locked and we walked in without knocking. It looked like a tornado had swept through the house. It was a mess; there were dirty clothes and dishes strewn all over the furniture and floor. Jessica was pacing back and forth, coming apart like a two-dollar watch. She looked 10 years older than she had when I'd last seen her. Her hair looked like a bird's nest and her face was thin and gaunt, mottled with anger and pain. Jayson's tousled red hair was matted and dirty as he sadly watched a blaring commercial on TV selling tampons. Brian wore unmatched pajamas with food stains on them and looked like an inpatient from a mental ward. He was on the floor, biting his nails. Both of the boys were as nervous as badly abused laboratory animals.

Jayson jumped up and ran towards me, greeting me like a long lost friend. My heart went out to him. He surprised me by hugging me tightly.

"Thank you so much for coming Mrs. Kirkpatrick. I don't know what to do for my mom. She's so sad." I hugged him and blinked back tears.

"You're welcome Jayson. I'll do what I can to help."

"You're her only friend. I didn't know who else to call." He sniffled and wiped his nose with his shirt sleeve.

Jessica ran over to me, crying, and grabbed me. "Judy, I just don't know what to do! I can't handle this!" She was sobbing and she completely ignored Jayson. I had never seen her so unglued. "I want to die!"

"Jessica, let's go to your room. Come on." I took charge and she was as docile as a baby and followed me to her room. The bed was unmade and there was a half-empty bottle of wine on the dresser. I ordered her to lie down and put a cold rag on her forehead. She babbled about how Josh had ended things, telling her she was too old for him. She suspected there was "another woman" but she wasn't sure. I tried to comfort her but she was inconsolable. I could relate to her pain; I knew the consuming longing for someone who no longer wants you.

After I got her calmed down somewhat, I returned to the living room and turned the TV to a channel that was showing "Batman Returns". The Wilson boys told me they hadn't eaten so I fixed them hot dogs, the only food I could find. After I got them, along with Trevor, settled in front of the TV, I heard Jessica yelling so I quickly walked back to her room. She was on the phone, screaming. I noticed a tape recording device attached to the phone.

"You asshole! Fuck you Josh!" She was wide-eyed and hyper-ventilating. "He hung up on me, that son-of-a –bitch!" She threw the phone against the wall, where it broke into pieces, then started pacing again, holding intense, chattering conversations with herself.

"Jessica, were you taping that call?" I was puzzled and uneasy.

"What? Yes. I tape all of my calls. Didn't you know that Judy?" She looked at me as if she'd never seen me before.

I felt somewhat faint. "So you've taped OUR calls?!" My mind raced to some of our conversations in the past months, in which I had shared intimate details of my life with her.

"Yeah. I just do it in case I ever need . . . you know . . . . evidence of things."

"Evidence of WHAT?!" She was really creeping me out now.

She frowned and waved her hand in the air as if to wave away smoke.

"I don't know."

"So you've taped my conversations?" I was yelling now and feeling sweaty and shaky.

"It's no big deal. A lot of people do it." Now she was walking around the room picking things up and throwing them on the floor, as if she were looking for something. Grabbing a pair of sandals, she bent over and shoved them on her feet. I wondered why she wasn't on Prozac or something; wasn't there some kind of medicine for people who caused OTHER PEOPLE to be depressed?

"No big deal? Maybe not to you. What do you do with the tapes?"

"I don't know. Listen Judy, I need to go out for a few minutes. I'll be back soon." She grabbed her purse and keys. I felt like I was on a pair of roller skates and somebody had pushed me down a hill. Things were spinning out of control.

"Where are you going?" Now I was feeling panicky.

"I'll be right back. It's really important." She grabbed her keys and looked in the mirror and shook her head. "God I look like shit!"

"Are you going to Josh's house?" I demanded.

"Of course not! I'll be back in an hour. Please stay with the boys." She scuttled out of the room as if it were about to burst into flames. I ran after her.

"No Jessica ! Come back here. I can't stay! I have things to do at home." But she was too fast for me. As I made it through the front door her car sped away, tires squealing. I slammed the door hard, then kicked it. Here I was again, stuck in Jessica-Wilson land, right in the middle of her chaos. I shook my head and turned around, again reviewing the mess. I decided to clean; cleaning was always very therapeutic for me when I felt like things were out of control. I became a whirlwind, straightening, vacuuming. I rinsed all the dirty dishes and loaded the dishwasher. Then I began poking through drawers, looked for tapes of phone calls. I didn't find any, which pissed me off. I was hoping to discover and confiscate the ones labeled "Judy Kirkpatrick bitching about her job" or "Judy Kirkpatrick having bad PMS!"

I read Jessica's papers, furtive and secretive, like a convict tunneling out of prison. After exhausting my search, I flopped on the sofa to watch "Knightrider" with the boys. By 10:00 pm, Jessica was still not home and I was exhausted. I put the Wilson boys to bed, after praying with them. In spite of my anger, I tried to be a calm, warm presence for them. They were so worried and upset about Jessica; I felt so sorry for them. I wondered if they would be better off living with Nicholas. Even if everything negative Jessica said about him was true, he still seemed to be the lesser of two evils!

Later, Trevor and I settled on opposite ends of the sofa. It's hard, cold leather reminded me of Jessica. I preferred my own sofa, soft and comforting. Trevor immediately went to sleep. I loved to watch him when his eyes were closed; his eyelashes were long, black and spidery and his breathing was even and calm. His presence was always somehow reassuring to me, like wrapping myself in a towel warm from the dryer. I was still edgy and felt homesick, like I was stuck at summer camp and had been away from home too long. I thumbed through a Vogue magazine, irritated by the numerous cardboard subscription invitations in it. I went to the last page, then began flipping forward, ripping out the cards in annoyance. Jessica came in just then and threw her keys on the counter. She slowly walked over and sat in a chair across from me, looking exhausted but much calmer. She softly told me that she was fine now and said she'd be okay. She thanked me politely for coming over, as if we were guests at a garden party. I woke Trevor and we stumbled tiredly out to the car. When we got home, Trevor fell asleep with his clothes on. His unfinished homework was piled on the kitchen table along with my unfinished writing homework. I forgot to set my alarm and fell into a deep, dreamless sleep.

The next day I awoke, cranky and irritable as I scrambled to get some breakfast together. I was so mad at Jessica I felt like throttling her. Again, I had let Jessica take up my time and drain me. Trevor had to go to school without his homework done which really pissed me off. When I arrived at work, breathless and frustrated, Freddie called seconds after I sat down at my desk.

"Judy, did you hear what Jessica Wilson did?"

Alarm bells went off in my head. "What now?"

"Last night she climbed up on Josh's balcony and turned on the gas grill, then she slit his tires! His neighbor saw it all and called Josh and the police."

I felt unmoored. "Oh my God, Freddie! I was at her house last night, watching her boys. I knew she was acting nuts but I couldn't stop her when she insisted she had to go out. I had no idea what she was doing!"

"Josh has taken out a restraining order on her. You've GOT to stay away from her this time. I mean it; she's very dangerous Judy!"

"I will Freddie. I really mean it this time. This is the last straw!"

"It's GOT to be. You've got to stop putting other people before yourself. It never works out. You're going to get hurt and Trevor isn't safe either!" he warned. After I hung up, I leaned my head back against the chair and closed my eyes. I was completely, totally sick of Jessica Wilson. I wished I'd never, ever met her.

For the next few weeks I wouldn't take any calls from Jessica again, trying to figure out how to handle this. I truly was afraid of her, and didn't want her mad at ME; after what she'd done to Josh, I knew that rejecting her could be really dangerous. I was worried sick about her boys. Finally, in desperation, I called Nicholas Wilson at his office and told him I was very concerned about Jessica and the boys. Nicholas sounded tired and stressed out and was rather abrupt with me. He said he was "working on it" but couldn't do much about it at the moment. I hung up feeling even more frustrated. I was kind of angry at him for not taking me more seriously. *Well, I thought, I tried to warn you. Later I would recall this conversation and wish that I had been more assertive. Maybe things would have turned out differently!*

The next day on my lunch hour I wandered around the beautiful, elegant stores in the plaza where my office was located. I hardly noticed the enticing elegant clothes and pricey furniture that I usually loved to linger over. I stopped at a beautiful fountain with multi-colored sprays of water shooting up into the air, like a rainbow against the sun. All morning I had been totally preoccupied with Jessica again. I needed to be sharp and witty on the phone but I was getting more and more distracted. I had accidentally hung up on Mr. Paul, a sweet elderly man who was one of my favorite customers. Jessica had been leaving messages on my home phone recorder and also at work, begging me to call her, saying she was a mess. I had considered changing my phone number but I knew that wouldn't stop Jessica; she would just barge into my home again.

When I got back to my desk and discovered she had called three more times, I put my head down on my desk and cried. I was so worn out with her. I prayed for a solution, some answer from God, how to handle this. Then a lightbulb went on. Margie! I could send her to Margie, my amazing therapist. Maybe she could help Jessica. It was more than obvious to me that Jessica's problems were too deep and complex for me to solve.

I called Margie and told her about Jessica. She was a little hesitant but then agreed to see her. I called Jessica and she was so glad I'd called her, she thanked me profusely. I almost felt guilty for abandoning her in the past weeks. But I knew she'd given me no choice. I said nothing about what I'd heard she had done to Josh; I didn't even want to get into that discussion. After I hung up I felt very relieved and hopeful that maybe she really would get some professional help and leave me the hell alone.

Two days later, Margie called me and was very upset. "I never want that woman in my office again!" she snapped. "And I strongly advise you to stay away from her Judy. She's impossible!"

"Margie, I'm so sorry!" I felt terrible for sending Jessica to her. I couldn't believe it; I'd never known Margie to lose her cool. Apparently Jessica had been rude and obnoxious and Margie would have none of her nonsense. That same day, Jessica left me a message saying that Margie hadn't been the least bit helpful. I felt like calling her and ripping her to shreds! I felt like I had finally "hit bottom" with her. But I knew I had to be careful; she was so unpredictable and obviously dangerous. I dialed her number with shaking hands and when she answered, I told her I was really sick and would not be able to see her for a while. I said I was sorry that she was having so many problems but that I couldn't keep trying to help her. It was making me physically sick, which was true. My Chronic Fatigue always got worse when I was under stress. I felt bad for the boys but I knew I couldn't endanger myself or my son any longer by being around her. She was crying when I hung up.

I called the guard gate in front of my condo and instructed them not to let Jessica in, under any circumstances. I was still worried about the Wilson boys and in a last-ditch attempt to help them I called Nicholas Wilson again. He sounded depressed, almost hopeless, and said again that he was "working on it."

He sighed deeply and thanked me for calling. I wracked my brain, trying to think of someone else I could call, but I came up empty; no one I knew even LIKED Jessica! I thought about calling Children's Services but I was afraid of what Jessica would do to me if she found out. I vowed that Jessica Wilson was no longer going to be part of my life.

CHAPTER NINE

He Said / She Said

Sometime in the fall of 1991, I had to go to the Scottsdale County Courthouse on my day off to renew my car registration. As I stood in a line of people in the Clerk's office, I could hear the annoying buzz of a drill down the hall where some construction was being done and I inhaled the wax polish on the linoleum floor and the overly sweet perfume from a woman in front of me.

I started to feel nauseated so I quickly took care of my business and hurried to get out of the building for some fresh air. As I stepped off the elevator on the first floor, someone hailed me.

"Judy!" I turned and saw Dena, a friend of mine who worked in the Clerk of Court's office. Dena was a tall, attractive woman in her early 40s with short brown hair. She had several manila files in her hands. I was happy to see her and we hugged. She had warm brown eyes and was always really upbeat. We had become friends because our boys had played softball on the same team for a couple of years. We talked for a few minutes and caught up with each other's lives. Then she glanced at her watch.

"Listen, I've got to get back to my desk. Oh, by the way, that woman who looks like you . . . Jessica? She's here today, in court with her ex-husband again. I saw them going into one of the courtrooms on the third floor. She looked pretty upset."

"Really? Thanks for telling me." I replied, as I wondered what the Wilsons were fighting about now. After saying goodbye to Dena, I stood there for a minute thinking about Jessica. I knew I should just leave but my curiosity got the better of me. I climbed the back stairs to the third floor and peeked out to make sure Jessica wasn't in the hall. I didn't see any sign of her so I slipped through a back door of the area near the courtrooms and found Johnny, a friend from AA. Johnny's wrinkled face reminded me of a cheerful prune. He had been a court bailiff for years and I knew he would be able to help me. He greeted me warmly and we shot the breeze for a minute. I told him I was curious about Jessica's case and he nodded and put his finger over his mouth, indicating for me to be quiet.

"Follow me," he whispered as he tiptoed to a door that led into one of the courtrooms and opened it slightly. I followed him and looked inside. Jessica and Nicholas Wilson and their respective attorneys were seated at tables in front of a heavy-set female judge. Jessica wore an old pair of beige slacks and a plain, cheap looking but low-cut white top. I realized her game immediately. She was trying to look "poor", otherwise she would have been wearing one of her many designer outfits. Nicholas Wilson wore an expensive looking blue suit and he was heavier than he had been the last time I'd seen him. He looked tired as he cleaned his thick glasses with a handkerchief. His attorney was a distinguished man in his 60s with silver hair. Jessica's attorney, a middle-aged man wearing a bad hairpiece was addressing the judge.

"Your Honor, as I said, Mrs. Wilson needs an increase in her child support to maintain expenses for her boys . . ."

"Bullshit!" yelled Nicholas. "Jessica Wilson needs to get a job! She does nothing all day but cause trouble!"

The judge frowned and shook her finger at him. "Now Nicholas, you know the rules."

Johnny and I both had to hold back our laughter. "Right on Nicholas!" I wanted to yell. Nicholas's face was red with anger but he ducked his head sheepishly as he put his glasses on. "Sorry Your Honor".

She smiled at him indulgently; it was clear that she liked or at least respected Nicholas. She turned back towards Jessica's attorney. "Continue Mr. Nelson."

Mr. Nelson smiled. "Thank you, Your Honor. As I was saying, my client needs more money from Mr. Wilson."

"If I may, Your Honor", said Nicholas's attorney, raising his hand.

The judge nodded. "Go ahead, Mr. Dennison."

"We feel that Jessica Wilson is already receiving more than sufficient support funds from Nicholas Wilson. She receives $900 a month in alimony and $1200 a month child support, plus she drives an almost new BMW given to her by Mr. Wilson."

"That sounds quite generous to me," said Judge Baker. Jessica's eyes narrowed and she opened her mouth to speak but her attorney grabbed her arm and shook his head.

Atty. Dennison went on, "As part of their divorce settlement Mrs. Wilson also received half of Mr. Wilson's 125,000 shares of Seaco, Inc. and half of his $27,000 interest in a local realty company."

When I heard all that I shook my head and Johnny nodded and rolled his eyes. God, to think about all the times she claimed she had no money and whined about her divorce. My ex-husband only had to pay me $240 a month and he was $50,000 behind! This was sickening.

"Mrs. Wilson, every day I see before me many women who have to make do with much less money than you, yet you continue to bog down my court with requests for more!" Judge Baker spoke to Jessica as if she were scolding a naughty child. She shuffled through some papers and her eyes narrowed as she read them. "I see that you were a legal secretary for 13 years before you were married. I don't understand why you haven't gone back to work, especially since you are more than qualified. Do you have some impediment keeping you from being employed?"

The judge's sarcasm was not lost on me.

Jessica looked furious for a moment but quickly switched to her sweet, innocent persona.

"Your Honor, I'm a single parent and it takes a lot of time and energy, being there for my boys."

"Aren't your boys in school Mrs. Wilson?"

"Well, yes, of course, but I need to be there when they get home."

The Judge frowned as she again looked through some papers. "You have one son, Jayson, who is 7 years old. And Brian is 5. Is that correct?"

"Yes Your Honor." Jessica nodded.

"Well, I see no reason why you can't get a job. Children of that age certainly don't need their mother to "take care of them" all day. There are after-school programs for working parents that the boys could go to. Motion for an increase of support money is denied. What else?"

Jessica practically stuck her tongue out when the judge turned away from her. I could see her clenching her fists and I had to smirk. So Miss Lazy Bones had to get a job like the rest of the world!

"Your Honor, if I may," said Atty. Dennison. "Mr. Wilson is seeking full custody of the boys. We feel that Jessica Wilson is unstable and is an unfit parent."

"Why you son-of-a-bitch!" screamed Jessica.

Judge Baker pounded her gavel. "Mrs. Wilson you will not disrupt this Court again!"

"Sorry Your Honor", said Jessica meekly.

"Your Honor, we bring to your attentions a restraining order brought against Mrs. Wilson by Atty, Josh Swanson. Mrs. Wilson dated Mr. Swensen and when he ended the relationship, she slit his tires, broke into his home and turned on a gas grill and made harassing phone calls to his place of employment. We feel that she is incapable of being the custodian of the boys."

"My God, that's terrible!" Judge Baker stared at Jessica, who squirmed uncomfortably.

"I might consider that type of behavior understandable in a troubled teenager but you are a 43 year old woman Mrs. Wilson. What do you have to say for yourself?"

"Your Honor, I know it was wrong. I was just out of my mind with grief and pain. Have you ever been jilted Judge? It hurts terribly!"

Judge Baker shook her head in disgust, looked at Atty. Dennison.

"Anything else counselor?"

"Yes Your Honor. When Atty. Wilson's father was gravely ill, in 1988, he was in a hospital in Birmingham, Alabama. While the family stood vigil beside his bed, Jessica Wilson made repeated calls to the nurses' station at all hours, using false excuses that the boys were ill or injured, to find out Mr.

Wilson's condition. Furthermore, when Nicholas Wilson Sr. passed away, later that year, Jessica showed up at his funeral wearing a white mini-dress and caused a commotion, greatly upsetting the grieving family."

Judge Baker snorted loudly. "Unbelievable! This is better than a soap opera."

"She also disrupted a private Wilson family gathering at Christmas later that year. Relatives say she came uninvited and ranted and raved for almost an hour, using profanity, then left the two boys outside in front of the house and took off in her car."

"That's right Your Honor." Nicholas spoke up. "It took me and my sister three hours to get the boys calmed down."

"What about HIM!" screamed Jessica. "He sent the boys home in a taxi!"

"Shut UP Mrs. Wilson!" Judge Baker screamed back. Jessica looked like she would like to tear the judge to shreds.

"My damn car wouldn't start!" yelled Nicholas. He was breathing so hard I was afraid he was going to have a heart attack. "Jesus! Listen to her Judge! I just don't understand the intensity of her anger. It's like a "Fatal Attraction" scenario."

"You asshole!" screamed Jessica as she jumped up and lunged towards Nicholas. Atty. Springer blocked her way.

"That is enough!" thundered Judge Baker. "One more outburst from either Mr. or Mrs. Wilson and I will hold you both in contempt of court and send you to jail, do you understand?"

"You tell 'em Judge!" Johnny chimed. Everyone in the room turned towards us and Johnny put his hand over his mouth, realizing his mistake. "Sorry Judge!"

"Johnny, you again!" Judge Baker yelled. "Get the hell out of here. And who is that woman with you . . ."

"Judy, what are you doing here?!" Jessica called, her eyes wide. I didn't stick around for more; I hightailed it out of there, down the back stairs and out to my car in record time. I was awash with embarrassment, like a Peeping Tom caught looking in someone's window. As I pulled out of the Courthouse parking lot, my hands were shaking. I forced myself to take some deep breaths and shook my head. What was the matter with me? Why did I even care about what Jessica was up to? As I drove home I was deeply grateful that Jessica was no longer part of my life; I assured myself that our "connection" had been broken. *I ALMOST CONVINCED MYSELF IT WAS TRUE.*

These Dreams (Go On When I Close My Eyes)

It was two weeks before Christmas and I was sitting on the plush, carpeted floor in my living room wrapping gifts. As I listened to Elvis Presley singing "Blue Christmas" on my favorite oldies station, I inhaled the fresh scent of pine needles from the Christmas tree Trevor and I had put up the night before. My cup of hot cocoa laced with cinnamon tasted exquisite.

Trevor came bounding in through the front door, bursting with excitement. "Christmas vacation has officially started. Yes!" He threw his backpack on the floor and walked over and gave me a kiss. I smiled; his enthusiasm was contagious. The Scottsdale Prep School was difficult for him; many of his classmates had started there in Kindergarten and were far ahead of him since he had just started in 7th grade. We had been spending many nights and weekends struggling over his homework together, so "Christmas Break" was a break for me too. He fixed himself a peanut butter and jelly sandwich and a glass of milk and sat down next to me, rummaging through a box of tree ornaments.

"Here's this new one from Grandma Kirkpatrick. It's got 1991 in gold lettering." He touched the beautiful glass bell. My ex-husband's mother sent us an ornament every year with the date on it. "I feel sorry for Jayson and Brian Wilson," he sighed as he played with a paper-weight, shaking it and making it "snow".

A rush of apprehension came over me. "Why?"

"Their mom and dad are having a really bad fight again."

"That's sad," I replied.

"Yeah, Jayson said that sometimes the police have to be there when their dad picks them up."

"God, that's terrible!" I wondered what was going to become of the Wilson boys, having a selfish mother like Jessica. I wished the best for them but I was not going to put myself in a position again to get hurt. Jessica was just too toxic and weird for me. I had consistently refused her invitations to get together for the past few months, telling her my health was bad.

And it was true; being with her made me quite ill!

That afternoon I slipped on my sea-blue bathing suit and cotton cover-up, grabbed a big, thick towel and went down to the pool. As I stepped outside, the air was crisp and stimulating. I swam laps for 30 minutes; the water was as warm as a bathtub and soothing to my tense muscles. While resting on the side of the pool doing leg kicks, I was joined by my neighbors, Mark and Mary Jo O'Halleron. Silver-haired and handsome, Mark was the Headmaster at the prep school Trevor was attending and Mary Jo, his attractive blond wife, was his assistant.

"Judy, we had another Jessica Wilson episode yesterday," Mark said as he did some leg stretches.

"What now?" I really didn't want to hear this, did I?

Mary Jo rolled her eyes. "Apparently Jayson got a "D" in science class and Jessica came into the office, screaming and carrying on, blaming his teacher. It was ridiculous."

"Yeah," Mark added. "I've dealt with these eccentric and demanding rich people for years but Jessica Wilson is the worst. She really is crazy, isn't she?"

"I think so." I got out of the pool; I just didn't need to have Jessica on my mind again. I'd been trying so hard to detach from her. As I dried off vigorously with my towel, we chatted about books and films; I always found their conversation interesting. They said they were going to Boston for the holidays and wished me a "Merry Christmas" and I left.

Trevor and I spent a quiet New Year's Eve watching movies and eating popcorn. I felt peaceful and serene, glad Jessica was no longer in our lives. Trevor missed the boys but he understood why he couldn't hang around with them anymore. I went to sleep early and was awakened at midnight by fireworks across the street. Smiling, I wished myself a "Happy New Year" and fell back to sleep.

One day in January of 1992, I stopped at the open-air fruit stand down the street from my condo. Fruits and vegetables of all colors were stacked neatly in wooden bins and the place smelled deliciously of oranges and flowers. I picked up several firm, ripe tomatoes and some bananas. At the checkout counter, I took a sample of warm pita bread covered with apple butter. As I savored the tasty food, Carol, the owner, rang up my order. She was in her 30s with short brown hair and she reminded me of the energizer bunny; she was so hyper she practically bounced in place.

"Hey Judy, your friend Jessica was in here yesterday!"

"Oh, was she?" Great, I thought. I really needed to hear about her today.

"Yeah. God, I still can't get over how much she looks like you. She said somebody robbed her and she had to buy a gun, for protection."

"A gun?" The food suddenly tasted like sawdust.

"Yeah. Apparently she had some guy who was doing maintenance work for her pick one up for her. God, you just aren't safe anywhere these days, are you?"

"No, I guess not." I felt sick.

"I wouldn't know how to use a gun." Carol went on as she gave me my change.

"Me either."

"Jessica does. She said she's been taking shooting lessons from some cop friend of hers."

"Oh, really?" I walked out quickly and jumped into my car and locked it. Driving home, a feeling of impending doom hung over me.

On February 7, 1992, in the early afternoon, I went grocery shopping at The Safeway Supermarket. As I was slowly making my way down the crowded produce aisle, I ran right into Jessica and the boys. She wore khaki slacks and a white halter top; she looked thin and there were dark circles under her eyes. In spite of my putting her off for months, she seemed happy to see me, she was all but wagging her tail. In fact, she greeted me as if we were family that had been separated during the war! I felt guilty again, that I had pushed her away and lied to her about being seriously ill. I was certain she knew that I had exaggerated my condition but she didn't mention it. She nervously chatted about taking the boys for a haircut earlier. The boys were polite, as always; Jayson was shy and tentative as he inquired about Trevor and asked me to have Trevor call him. I felt truly sad when I saw the longing on his face. The Wilson boys were just innocent victims in this never-ending drama. When we parted, I told Jessica that I'd call her, but we both knew I didn't mean it. It bothered me; I hated "phony" conversations. But I felt like I'd been backed into a corner and had no way out. I thought about the gun Jessica had purchased and wondered if it was in her purse.

That night I had a lot of trouble getting to sleep. For some strange reason my house felt whispery and dark, like the walls were breathing heavily. I finally fell into a restless doze at 11:30 pm and dreamed a series of weird and disturbing scenarios in which Nicholas and Jessica were viciously screaming at each other. Everything was fuzzy and out of focus at first; all I could hear was their fighting. Then, slowly, a blood drenched knife appeared, then Jayson came into focus. He was very frightened and kept pleading with his parents to stop fighting. The last thing I remembered was Jayson's face; he looked tortured and devastated. I lurched awake, shaky and nauseous. I tried to calm my nerves by listening to my "Louise Hay" soothing meditation tape; her soft, hypnotic voice with the waves crashing in the background helped a little.

In the morning, sluggish and cranky, I gulped down three cups of coffee while Trevor ate toaster waffles. When the phone rang, I jumped nervously, as if a guillotine blade had just dropped.

"Judy, I have some very bad news." Freddie spoke slowly, as if the words were boulders weighing him down.

I shivered, as if I'd just been rescued from an icy river. A heavy sinking feeling came over me and I sat down, clutching the receiver with shaking hands. "What happened?"

CHAPTER ELEVEN

Through the Eyes of a Child; Jayson Wilson's Story

(The following testimony was given by Jayson Wilson to the Scottsdale police on the night of February 7, 1992 regarding what had transpired that day)

Well the day started out pretty much like any other day. Me and my brother went to school. Then Mom picked us up after school and we got our hair cut. My mom was kind of mad, like she always was lately. I mean, ever since Josh broke up with her she was really mad and sad and she cried a lot. So, anyway, we went grocery shopping at Safeway and we ran into Mrs. Kirkpatrick. She was nice to us but I felt really sad because I knew she didn't want to be friends with my mom anymore and that reminded me that Trevor couldn't hang out with me anymore either. That made me pretty mad at my mom; it just wasn't fair.

"Later that day, at about 5:00, my mom was on the phone talking really nice to someone when Dad pulled up in our driveway. Brian and I were so happy! We hadn't seen him for a long time. My mom told us to go in our room and pack our bags because we would be spending the weekend at Dad's. So we went into our room and started packing. Even though I was excited about seeing Dad I was kind of nervous because . . . well . . . they had been fighting really bad lately and I was afraid that something was going to happen.

"When I was looking for some clean socks, I heard Dad's car door shut and then I heard a noise so I looked out the bedroom door and saw Dad walking down the hallway. Mom was scrunched against the wall and she was screaming at Dad. Then she pulled a gun from the waist of her pants and aimed it at him! I felt like I was going to be sick; I couldn't believe what I was seeing!

"Dad said, "What is that?" and he started running towards Mom. She stood on her toes with her back against the wall and held the gun close to her body and fired the gun at him! It sounded like a bomb exploding, it was so loud, and I saw flashes of bright light. Dad spun around after the bullet hit him and the glass in the door behind him broke. I could hear sounds of glass falling all around. Then she fired at him again and he fell really hard on the floor. There was blood all over his white shirt. I was screaming and so was my brother, who was behind me. I tried to stand in front of him so he wouldn't see what was going on.

"Mom yelled at me to get back in my room. I went back in and I slammed the door shut but there was a hole where the doorknob used to be, so I peeked through it to watch. Then she shot him again! My little brother got in the closet behind me and he was crying real loud. I looked at Dad, lying on the floor, and I felt worse than I ever had in my life. I knew inside me that he was probably already dead, but I felt like I should try to do something to help him! I felt like I was going crazy. There was something glary in his hand but I couldn't tell what it was. I was just about to leave my room to go out and see if he might still be alive, but Mom's voice came on the intercom and she yelled, "You boys stay where you are!" I felt like I was watching the scariest horror movie; I just couldn't understand why she shot him!

"I ran to the phone in my room and dialed "911" and when the operator answered I said there's been a shooting at 45 Cactus Drive in Scottsdale! Please come quickly!"

"While I was talking, my mom got on the other extension phone and started punching in some numbers, trying to call someone. She kept saying "Jimmy, pick up!" Then she heard the operator's voice and said "Who is this? Who is this?" When she found out I had the 911 operator on the line, she started crying hysterically and said "Nicholas Wilson was coming up the hallway with a knife and I shot him. I don't know if I got him or not . . . I'm in the bedroom and I've got my finger on the door. My kids are in the closet. I've got a gun." Then she hung up the phone. The phone started ringing right away and it rang and rang but she wouldn't answer it and she yelled at me not to answer it. Finally, after about five minutes, she answered it and she was crying really hard. After that she came into the bedroom with us and she got down on the floor on her back and braced the door shut with her feet and told us to stay back. She was crying hysterically. The last thing I remember was sirens . . . so many sirens . . . getting louder and louder as they came towards our house."

CHAPTER TWELVE

A Funeral for A Friend

Nicholas Wilson's funeral mass was held on February 11th at St. Edwards Church in Scottsdale. The sky was unusually moody and dark as I walked in with Connie. She had gone to high school with Nicholas. As we took our seats, people stared at me as if I was naked and, belatedly, I realized that I should have disguised myself. Many of them probably thought I was Jessica! I was so upset today I really didn't even care what anyone thought.

Connie whispered, "Sweetie, you're gonna have to dye your hair blond or something!" If I hadn't been so sad and upset, I might have found a strange humor in the situation. There were beautiful and obviously expensive arrangements of flowers at the front by Nicholas's casket. The room was packed. Connie and I were able to get seats but quite a few people stood in the back and in the side aisles. Many of them were wealthy socialites who knew the Wilson family. A lot of them wept. Nicholas's family, including red-haired Doug Wilson, sat in the front row and wept openly.

Two of Nicholas's brothers spoke; both of them could hardly talk through their tears.

Nicholas's partner, Phillip Ward, gave one of the eulogies. He remembered Nicholas's younger days at Notre Dame, where he had been captain of the swim team. Ward said, "If you couldn't find Nicholas on a Friday night you only had to look at the paper to see where Notre Dame was playing." He also mentioned that Wilson "somewhat prophetically" had just made the last payment on his sons' college tuition pre-paid plan. Wilson said to Ward that day, "At least I've taken care of that."

When "Amazing Grace" was sung by an ample black woman with a voice like soft chocolate, there wasn't a dry eye in the room. I felt like I was in "The Big Chill"; so many yuppies were present, well dressed people in their 30s and 40s. In spite of the somber, sad atmosphere, I was strangely comforted. There was so much love and kindness in the room, you could almost see old grudges evaporating into the air like smoke. I fleetingly wondered if Jessica and Nicholas had been here today, maybe even they could have forgiven each other

CHAPTER THIRTEEN

Insomnia

If Andy Warhol was correct when he predicted that everybody has "15 minutes of fame", Jessica Wilson was getting a lot more than her share; in fact, she became an overnight celebrity! The shooting incident was not just on the local news; because it had happened to someone from a wealthy and well-known Scottsdale family, it was on national news.

Women everywhere who had parted badly from a difficult relationship wanted to see if she would get away with it. Men watched in fear, worried that it could happen to them.

I watched "Entertainment Tonight" a few days after Nicholas's funeral. A picture of Jessica and Nicholas from a party sometime in the 80s flashed on the screen. They were dressed in bathing suits and Hawaiian leis and were eating pineapple. They made a very striking couple and looked so happy. I felt a twinge of sadness and even empathy for Jessica. I, too, had started out my marriage optimistic and bubbly. But then, one day when I was eight months pregnant, I had been cleaning out a closet and found a box of "love letters" sent by a woman from Wisconsin to my husband. In reading them I discovered that Rob was planning to leave me after our child was born and go on the road with this woman, who was a singer. I was enraged and devastated! That night, when he came home drunk at midnight, we had a terrible fight and if I had had a gun, who knows what might have happened? I did throw a hairbrush at him and we screamed at each other for hours. So I could certainly imagine the anger and loss of control Jessica might have felt when she found out Nicholas was cheating on her. But to kill someone, to actually plan it and carry it out? I didn't really think I was capable of it; at least I hoped not.

The whole situation with Jessica being on TV was surreal. Usually I didn't watch the news at night because it tended to over-stimulate my brain and keep me up. But I had a sort of morbid fascination with her saga and couldn't seem to help myself. As I sipped my herbal tea, a young blond newscaster came on. She had suntan so dark, I could almost smell the Coppertone. She was broadcasting live from the yard in front of Jessica's house. "Scottsdale detectives are investigating the slaying of 42-year-old Nicholas Wilson, who was shot three times at close range with a .357 Magnum in the hallway of his ex-wife's home Friday. Jessica Wilson, age 43, claims that he was coming at her with an 8 inch knife and she shot him in self-defense. Nicholas Wilson was a prominent tax attorney from a Scottsdale law firm, Wilson, Ward, Lesher and Damon. Sources tell us that the couple had been bickering for several years over child support, alimony, visitation for their two boys and property division. Ten-year-old Jayson Wilson, the couple's oldest son, was watching from behind a bedroom door while his brother, Brian, age 8, hid in a closet. Juno Beach detectives will be taking the results of their investigation to the Grand Jury to determine whether or not Mrs. Wilson should be indicted.

"Mrs. Wilson's attorney, Gabriel Myers had this to say about his client as he stood on the steps in front of the Scottsdale County Courthouse." He wearing a silk suit and was as suave and confident as an actor as he faced the news cameras surrounding him. "The police have all the evidence to reflect self-defense, including 911 tapes of what happened at the scene. Jessica Wilson is innocent of any crime. She was forced to shoot her former husband. She is a victim in this tragedy! "

That really pissed me off and I yelled out loud, "Victim my ass! Jessica Wilson is always the victim!"

"Mom, why are you yelling?" Trevor stood in the doorway, rubbing his eyes and looking cranky and tired. "You're making too much noise! You woke me up!

"I'm sorry honey." I quickly turned off the TV, mad at myself. Great. The last thing I needed to do was wake Trevor up, especially on a school night. I glanced at my watch and saw that it was almost 11:00 pm. What was the matter with me anyway? I almost never stayed up this late. Damn Jessica!

I followed Trevor to his room. After I got him settled in bed, I read "Velveteen Rabbit" to him. Even though he was getting older, he liked it and it was one of my favorite children's stories and always made me think of how the people we love are not perfect; none of us are. We love each other in spite of, or because of, our flaws. I wondered if I loved Jessica? I had such conflicting emotions about her. Maybe part of me loved part of her? It was so confusing. At Trevor' request I sang "Hush Little Baby" and rubbed his back for a while. When he seemed to be asleep, I stood up to leave but he grabbed my hand.

"One more minute Mom, please!" he begged. I sat back down and started rubbing his back again. He smiled contently and his eyes closed. I watched his chest rise and fall as he took deep, even breaths. I sighed deeply. I felt like I was always rushing away from him, that he was always asking me for "one more minute" of my time. I thought of Millie, an elderly lady from my AA Women's Meeting, who always told us the story of when her son was little. She used to fret about his clothes being messy, his socks not matching; she was always telling him to "hurry". When he was 20 he was killed by a drunk driver. Years later, Millie still became overwhelmed with grief when she talked about him. Tears stung my eyes and I stroked Trevor's soft brown hair, thinking of how fragile life was. Finally I headed to bed myself.

An hour later I was still awake, staring at the ceiling. My body was tense and my mind was like a video game; bleeps of worry and regret kept popping back and forth, making it impossible to sleep. I contemplated calling my doctor the next day to see if I could get some Xanax. But I knew that would be a terrible mistake. I had been addicted to Xanax for a year and it had been hell coming off of it. The last thing I needed was to relapse! Damn Jessica! She was pushing me over the edge; even my job was suffering.

There was a new salesman, Evan, who was very aggressive and lately, a few of my regular customers had told me they were renewing their subscriptions with him. It made me angry and I couldn't figure out how he even got their names. I had been so preoccupied with all the shit about Jessica, I hadn't been at my best. I told myself to let it go, that tomorrow I would go in and take charge again. I had been the top salesperson for years, working very hard and long hours. I wasn't going to let some new guy come in and intimidate me, even if he did look like Sylvester Stallone! On top of that, I was way behind in my writing class and my damn hair was falling out from stress!

I closed my eyes and chanted to myself, "All is in Divine Order" but the image of Jessica and Nicholas kept interfering with my thoughts. I wondered if I could have done more to help, if I should have been more forceful when I called Nicholas to warn him about Jessica's behavior. I sometimes felt that I spoke too softly, that I didn't have enough power and strength in my voice to make people really listen to me. I always tried to listen to my instincts and it had been obvious for months that Jessica was out of control. Knowing how much she enjoyed "pulling one over" on people, I strongly suspected she had planned the whole shooting. I tossed and turned and the blankets got all tangled up in my legs. Furious, I sat up and tore them off and threw them on the floor. At 1:00 a.m. I marched into the kitchen and made myself a cup of "Sleepytime Tea". After drinking it, I got back in bed and put my headset on to listen to my "waves" tape but the batteries were dead! I gritted my teeth; I felt like screaming! Finally I fell into a fitful, restless sleep. The next thing I knew, Trevor was climbing into bed with me, kicking me and scratching me with his toenails. "Ow! Be careful!" I shoved his feet away from my legs.

"I had a bad dream about Mr. Wilson," he mumbled. I nodded and put my arm around him. It's going around kid, I thought to myself. We were like two exhausted boat refugees who were too tired to sleep but too tired to move.

The next morning I felt like a crabby, bloated robot as I forced myself to get ready for work. Trevor and I were both tired so I drove him to school. After dropping him off, I realized I was going to be late and I stepped on the accelerator. A block from the school, I passed the elderly crossing guard whose bright orange belt glowed like a neon sign. He frowned and shook his head and pointed his finger at me accusingly as I sped by him. Embarrassment flushed my face red and I slowed down. I knew this was going to be a long day.

When I got to work, I was rushing so much I almost locked my keys in the car. I quickly walked up the stairs and tripped, stubbing my toe. "Dammit!" I hobbled up the rest of the stairs. When I opened the door to my private office, I was shocked to see Evan sitting at my desk, going through my drawers.

"What the hell are you doing Evan?" I demanded. My adrenaline was racing; I was ready for a fight. He casually pushed the top desk drawer closed, not at all concerned that he was caught going through my desk.

He flashed me a smile. "I was just checking to see if you had an extra headset. Mine isn't working."

"Oh really?" I stomped over to a nearby cabinet and took a headset out of it and threw it down in front of him. "You're looking in the wrong drawer Evan."

"Am I?" He still made no move to get up.

"Yes! Unless you're trying to steal my customer lists!"

"Judy, chill out! Don't be so paranoid. Are you okay? You seem upset."

"Yes no...I don't know." I sighed deeply and sank down in a chair across from him, completely out of steam. "This shit about Jessica Wilson is really wearing me out."

"I'll bet." He looked very concerned and I instantly felt bad that I had been so suspicious of him. He wasn't a bad guy. In fact, during the few weeks he'd been working here, he had often expressed concern for my health and had even brought me some articles about homeopathic remedies for chronic fatigue. Maybe I was being too hard on him, taking my anger at Jessica out on him.

"Anyway Evan, you're welcome to use my headset. I don't like it; it always gets caught in my hair."

"Okay, thanks. And take it easy. You can't let Jessica's problems make you crazy."

"Yeah, you're right." I was so exhausted I felt like I was going to pass out.

He ran his hand through his thick, dark wavy hair. "Do you need some help with your sales calls? I'm caught up." I hesitated. I hated to share my customer lists. I was very competitive and driven to perfection when it came to my job. It had been hard since I'd been sick, to keep up with it all. He looked so eager. Truthfully, I was behind on my calls.

I said, "Give me a minute and I'll bring you in a few names. I could use your help with the four week trials."

He frowned and sighed, then shrugged his shoulders. The four-week trial customers were a hard sell and they were less likely to renew than many of my long time, tried and true customers. But that's all I was willing to share with him. He left, closing the door quietly.

The headset was still on my desk. I shook my head, realizing that he had never intended to borrow it; he had probably stolen some names already! I could smell his Brut aftershave and it made me nauseous. I sat in my chair and put my head down on the desk, feeling like the weight of the world was on my shoulders. I felt totally drained, like my batteries were dead. I was at my limit, from all the chaos that Jessica had brought into my life and because I was so sleep-deprived. People confused me sometimes; they wore me out. I felt like I needed a quiet vacation somewhere all by myself.

I went in to see Rick, my brother who was also my boss. Rick was always a friend, always kind and understanding. His green eyes behind his wire-rimmed glasses showed concern as I told him what was going on with Jessica and Evan.

"Judy, you know I always believe we should go with the flow." His voice was enthusiastic yet calming at the same time. "You're obviously exhausted. Don't fight it. Why don't you get as much done as you can this morning and then take the afternoon off? You don't need to worry about your sales. You're the best salesperson we've got. I'll talk to Evan; just forget him." He gave me a bear hug and I left his office feeling much better. Rick was always good at soothing my ruffled feathers. I worked all morning and actually got quite a few sales. At noon, I left and forced myself to go to the grocery store since we hardly had any food in the house. Safeway wasn't crowded but some of the customers who were there looked at me strangely. I couldn't figure it out at first; I was so tired I really didn't care. When I got to the checkout counter, the young cashier glared at me until she saw the name on my check. Then she looked relieved.

"God, I thought you were someone else."

Of course, I realized; they all thought I was Jessica Wilson. I nodded wearily. "I know. People always think I'm her."

"Did you hear she took her boys and went into hiding?" she asked as she bagged my groceries.

"No, I didn't know that." God, what next? Would all this crap ever end?

"Yeah. They had it on the news this morning. There's a warrant out for her arrest."

No wonder everyone was staring at me! They were probably ready to call the cops! I made a mental note to myself; buy a blond wig and start wearing it! On the drive home I turned on the radio to listen to some music but the news was on. I was about to turn it off when I heard Jessica's name mentioned. "Jessica Wilson was ordered by Judge Howard Berman not to talk about the murder case with her boys. The State Department of Health and Rehabilitative Services tried to take custody of the boys from Mrs. Wilson but the judge ruled that they had not presented enough evidence to prove the boys should be placed in foster care. The judge gave HRS seven hours to refile. Scottsdale Detective Stephen Ramirez has told us that Mrs. Wilson has gone into hiding with her boys. Mrs. Wilson's attorney, had this to say. "Jessica Wilson is an excellent parent. Any unbiased individual with knowledge of the family would happily agree with me."

I turned the radio off, shaking my head. Knowing Jessica as I did, I was sure she'd coerce and poison the boys to lie for her. I recalled the way she marked their wrists at Art Fest so they could sneak in. I felt like calling the judge and tattling on her! But of course I wouldn't; in fact I planned to stay as far away from the whole ordeal as possible. An "excellent parent?" I knew Jessica loved her boys but her behavior was so erratic and sometimes bizarre. I shoved in a Don Henley cassette and he was singing "The Heart of the Matter". The song was about "Forgiveness", one of my favorite songs. Tears filled my eyes. I knew I had to try and let this anger towards Jessica go; it was affecting my serenity and health.

When I got to the condo, there were no grocery carts available which irritated me; people sometimes left them in the halls if they were too lazy to return them to the little room next to the parking garage. I had bought a lot of food and had to take the bags two or three at a time and leave them by the front door. When I got to the elevators, one was on "hold" because a resident was moving in furniture. The other elevator had been hung up several floors above. I shook my head, feeling quite sorry for myself, and carried three bags up the stairs to the 8th floor. When I came back down to get the rest of them, Fran, one of my neighbors, a middle -aged, perpetually crabby women, was standing next to them, frowning.

"You know you're not supposed to leave things in front of the door!"

She scolded.

"Who are you? The Door Police?" I snapped at her. "There was no damn shopping cart! Get a life!"

She'd picked the wrong day to mess with me.

"You are so rude!" she yelled back. "You are exactly why I hate young people living here. Why I am just . . ."

"Whatever!" I shouted and grabbed the remaining two bags of food and walked away from her, back to the stairwell. After climbing the 8 floors again and putting away the groceries I decided to lie down and rest for a few hours before I picked Trevor up from school for softball practice. I was so glad I had the afternoon off; I was completely frazzled. As I headed for my bedroom, the phone rang. I almost didn't answer it but worried it might be important. Wearily I headed back to the kitchen.

Judy, it's me!" Jessica! Dammit! "Judy, listen, this is very important. I need you to be a character witness for me in court. It's terribly important Judy. It's life or death!"

I had to think fast and all I came up with was my standard excuse. "Jessica, I'm really sick. That's why I'm home right now. I don't think . . . ."

"Judy please! I need your help. I'm going to give you a number and you can't tell anyone you heard from me. Whatever you do, don't give this number to anyone. Call me tonight!" She recited a local phone number and I wrote it on my hand because I couldn't find a piece of paper. She insisted I read the number back to her. I got her off the phone by promising to call her later, although I had no intention of calling her back. After I hung up, I stood in the middle of the kitchen, wondering what to do next. I thought about calling the police but quickly discarded the idea. I knew now how dangerous Jessica was and I didn't want her mad at me. I went to my room to lie down but felt like I had drank 10 cups of coffee. A couple of hours later, not feeling any more rested at all, I went to pick Trevor up and drive him to practice. All the way there he was crabby.

"I don't want to go! Jayson Wilson doesn't have to play softball. It's not fair! I hate softball!"

"You were the one who wanted to join up. That's why I signed you on the team. Stop whining!"

"I'm not whining You stop whining! I hate you. You're so mean!"

"Stop it now. You don't really hate me. You're just tired. We both are."

"I'm not tired. I don't want to go and I mean it." His arms were crossed tightly across his chest.

"You're going to softball!"

"No I'm not! You're not the boss of me!"

"Just shut up!"

"YOU shut up! I wish Mrs. Wilson was my mother. She doesn't make them do all the stupid things you make me do."

"That's enough!" I pulled the car over to the curb. "Stop it right now. I mean it! Since we're both exhausted we'll skip practice just for tonight but you do not talk to me that way, do you understand?"

"Okay Mom. Sorry." Trevor leaned over and hugged me, his anger spent. I hugged him tightly, glad we were going home. I felt like I was going to collapse with exhaustion.

At home I warmed Trevor up a frozen pizza. Later, after I got him to bed, I drank a lot of Sleepytime Tea and winded down early. Just as I was ready to fall asleep, the damn phone rang. I went to the kitchen to listen to the answering machine.

"Judy, it's Jessica. Pick up, pick up! I know you're in there. I'm across the street at a phone booth and I can see your lights on!"

Busted. Damn her to hell! I grabbed the receiver. "What?!! What do you want Jessica?"

"Can we come and stay at your place for a few days? We don't have any place to hide.

Just for a couple of nights, please?"

Think fast, I told my poor brain-dead self. "Jessica," I whispered, "there's someone here . . ."

"Oh no! Who?"

"Troy!" I lied. Troy who hadn't called me in years.

"Oh, well . . . you can't be too sick if you let him come over. Call me at that number I gave you tomorrow when he leaves. It's my friend Betsy's number. Maybe we can stay with her for one more night. So make sure you call me Judy!"

"Oh yeah, I'll call." Right. Tomorrow I was definitely getting a new unlisted phone number! I hung up the phone and dragged myself to my bedroom. I knew another night of insomnia awaited me. My throat hurt, my head was pounding; I wondered how in the hell I would ever make it to work tomorrow. I cursed the day I'd met Jessica Wilson.

CHAPTER FOURTEEN

Deadly Sins

I slumped down in my car seat, peering over the dashboard, watching dozens of Sunday morning worshipers head into church on a steaming hot day. The service was scheduled to begin in 15 minutes and, so far, no sign of Jessica. For the past three weeks I had only made it as far as the parking lot, then turned around and gone home, in fear of running into her. But today I was feeling brave so I got out and headed inside. Trevor had gone rock climbing with some friends so I had the weekend to myself. I was greeted in the lobby by a cheerful young man wearing a navy blazer who handed me a program. In the crowded theater, I sat in a chair towards the back of the room next to an elderly woman with brightly rouged cheeks. Her heavy, powdery perfume reminded me of the scent worn by my grandma, who had been dead for years. I used to love spending the night at Grandma's house in the little town in Iowa where my parents had grown up as next-door neighbors and childhood sweethearts. A train would go by every night at 3:00 a.m. and I would wake up and hear it, comforted somehow, then sink back into a warm, deep sleep. Still to this day, whenever I heard a train, I would feel drowsy, like I needed a nap. Now, I listened to a young man with a ponytail softly strumming "You've Got a Friend" on an acoustic guitar. I felt grateful and happy. I had really missed coming to church. I had been watching Joyce Meyers, an evangelical preacher who my mom really liked, on TV, just to stay spiritually plugged in, even though her constant "Amen" and "Hallelujah" sometimes grated on my nerves.

For the past few weeks, I'd created a cocoon of isolation for myself, after changing my phone number to stop the calls from Jessica. I talked to Freddie and he strongly urged me to distance myself from her in every way possible. I quit reading the paper and listening to the news. I even asked my co-workers not to talk to me about Jessica's case.

Because of all my efforts to "Keep It Simple" like my 12th Step program advised, I was back into my writing, I was sleeping better and I felt much more calm and serene. Daily meditation had become part of my routine and I prayed to let go of my anger towards Jessica. But I wasn't taking any more chances of being mistaken for her so today I was wearing a cheap, tight blond wig that felt like a vise on my head and a baggy, unflattering dress. Wire-rimmed glasses irritated the bridge of my nose. They brought back a memory of being in 5th grade and hiding my dorky, thick brown glasses behind a bush on my way to school. I sighed deeply. It was so unfair; I had to sneak into my own church and disguise myself to go out in public. I couldn't even flirt with the cute guy I'd been admiring a few months ago; he wasn't going to recognize me this dowdy getup! Since I had donated $500 to the building fund for the new church that was under construction, I figured I should show up and get my money's worth. I was feeling rested but lonely too. I wished I had someone in my life to spend time with, go out to a movie or dinner. I checked my watch; five minutes before the service would start and I hadn't seen Jessica yet. I breathed a sigh of relief.

The woman next to me smiled and spoke in a loud whisper. "I'm Gladys Evans. I haven't seen you here before. Are you a new member?"

"Actually I've been coming off and on for a while. I'm Judy Kirkpatrick."

"Nice to meet you. Say, did you read the paper this morning about that Wilson woman who killed her ex-husband?"

"No, I didn't." Dammit! Here we go again.

"She's a member of this church. It's terrible!"

"Yes."

"Apparently they're saying his will is missing!"

"Really? That's strange. Wasn't he an attorney?" I sighed. God, what did I do wrong to be constantly punished like this?

"Very strange. He had copies of it in 3 or 4 places and they're all missing!" Gladys' voice was getting louder and louder and she looked excited, like someone watching the medics pulling a dead body out of a wrecked car.

"So what does that mean?" I said flatly. As if I gave a damn.

"She could have gotten control of the boys' inheritance but apparently Wilson's brother and sister knew what was in it and they got it reinstated."

"Good."

"The boys can't inherit any money until they're 35, so their greedy mother can't get her hands on it!"

Although I was sick of hearing about Jessica, I was glad to hear that she would not get Nicholas's fortune. Maybe there was some justice in this world after all.

"I'll bet she's furious." I offered, as it seemed that Gladys wanted to keep talking.

"I'm sure! Oh, also, she's claiming that he was '$60, 000 behind in child support. And she said that he ruined her credit by paying credit cards late."

My jaw dropped; there was no way Jessica would have let Nicholas get behind. She had never mentioned it to me in all the time we spent together. And she always had money for expensive clothing and for dining at trendy restaurants.

"I wouldn't believe anything she says!" I told Gladys.

"Yes! I hear she's crazy!" Gladys shook her head and rolled her eyes. I was saved from further discussion about Jessica when Pastor Luke got up on the stage to begin the service. My serenity was quickly slipping away and I thought about leaving, but I didn't; it would signify that I was again letting Jessica rule my life. I forced myself to pay attention as the pastor went through the announcements and then led the congregation in two songs. By the time he began the sermon, I had managed to relax and shake off the conversation with Gladys.

"Today I want to talk about the Seven Deadly Sins. Pride," he said, "is the excessive belief in one's own abilities that interferes with a person's recognition of the grace of God. Pride has been called the sin from which all others arise. Pride is also known as vanity." I thought about that. Vanity? I had to admit I was vain at time. I hated to go out in public without my makeup on. In fact, I hated the way I looked right now!

"Greed," he went on, "is a by-product of pride. Greed is the desire for material wealth or gain, ignoring the realm of the spiritual." I mulled that over. Greed? That was Jessica Wilson's driving force. I wasn't the least bit surprised that Nicholas's will was missing. I knew Jessica prided herself on her knowledge of the law; how many times had she bragged to me that she could outwit Nicholas and most attorneys she knew? She would have known where copies of the will were kept and she was certainly manipulative enough to find a way to obtain them. The pastor resumed his sermon, reading from Proverbs. "Don't let evil people worry you or make you jealous. They will soon be gone like the flame of the lamp that burns out." I wondered, is Jessica evil? Will she ever be gone from my life? I flashed back to 6th grade when I used to roller-skate every Friday night. I was a "goody two shoes" back then, clumsy, too tall, wearing braces and scared to death of boys. But there were these brothers – the Bloomer brothers – everyone called them "hoods". They wore black leather jackets and their hair was slicked back and they smoked in back of the roller skating rink. I used to watch them; they fascinated me. They oozed self-confidence; they weren't afraid of adults or anyone for that matter. My very first "crush" had been on the youngest Bloomer brother, Dale. I used to daydream of being his "chick", hip and cool, riding on the back of his motorcycle. Jessica reminded me of them. I had let her into my life because she fascinated me in that same, sick way; she was the "bad girl"; she said and did things I thought about but never had the nerve to do.

I shook my head, totally frustrated. I had come to church for peace and tranquility and here I was all upset again, giving Jessica free rent in my head. I obsessed for a few minutes about how nice a couple of Xanax would be right now, just to "take the edge off" the tension that had tightened all my muscles. I had to force the thought out of my head. I was damn sure not going to let her trigger me into a relapse; I had come too far to go back to that life. Forcing myself to sit through the rest of the service, I left, stopping for a quick trip to the restroom. As I fumbled to unlock my car, a hand grabbed me roughly on the shoulder and I spun around, coming face to face with a very angry Jessica! Her eyes were small, hateful slits and I was flattened against my car by the force of her rage. She was so close that I could see angry blue veins in her temples.

"I have a bone to pick with you Judy!" she snarled with such startling force that I flinched.

"What?" A creepy feeling spread over me as I realized I was looking into the face of a killer.

"Why the frigging hell did you call Nicholas at his office Judy? What were you up to?" Her voice was icy.

"I don't know what you're talking about." My heart was in my throat and for a moment, I went blank.

"Don't play that innocent crap with me Judy. I have proof that you called Nicholas."

"What proof?" I hedged, as several onlookers stopped to watch us.

"I saw his office notes. You called him two months ago. Why on earth would you call Nicholas? What was going on behind my back Judy?!"

I flashed back to my calls to Nicholas. I had totally forgotten the useless conversations with him. Quickly, my fear was replaced by fury.

"How dare you accuse me of anything you bitch!" I yelled.

She stepped back as if the wind had been knocked out of her.

"Jesus, Jessica! I was worried about you and the boys. You were talking about suicide! Do you have any idea how much pressure that put on me? I had to do something!"

Tears filled her eyes and her shoulders slumped. Her voice was soft and timid now. "But to call Nicholas . . . . you know how he hated me. You were just giving him more information to use against me Judy."

"I didn't know what else to do. I thought maybe he would help you."

"I'm sorry for jumping all over you Judy. Please forgive me."

It was blazing hot and uncomfortable. I had to get into my car and turn on the air-conditioning NOW! Then a verse from the Bible came to mind. "He maketh His sun to rise on the evil and the good, and sends rain on the just and the unjust." I was exhausted by my emotions. And sad; the mellow, happy feeling I'd come here today with was completely obliterated. "Whatever. How did you even recognize me?"

"Oh, I've been watching you sit in your car every week."

"Watching me? More like stalking me! What do I have to do, get a restraining order like Josh did? Is that what it's come to Jessica?"

"Judy, I would never stalk you. I thought we were friends. You don't know what it's like . . . all the publicity . . ."

"That's just it; I DO know! It's because of you that I have to disguise myself. Everywhere I go, people either think I'm you or your sister, after that stupid lie you circulated. You have no idea what it's like for ME! You don't think of anyone but yourself, ever. I'm sick of it; the whole situation."

"Judy, I'm sorry. I didn't even think about that. Is that why you're wearing that ugly wig?"

"Oh, no, I love looking like a wallflower Jessica!" I spat at her. I wanted to smack her.

"You changed your phone number. Why? You seem to hate me."

"I don't hate you Jessica. I'm just empty. I simply can't deal with your life anymore."

"Please Judy, give me another chance. Could we go to lunch and talk? You're my only friend."

Maybe it was because I had just left a worship service, or maybe I was just tired of being angry. But as I stared at Jessica, I felt pity for her. What would Jesus do? I wondered. I fought back tears of frustration. Sighing deeply, I hugged her. She clung tightly to me and I had to gently push her away.

"Listen, I hope things work out for you. I really do. But I have to stay away from you." "Would you at least call me Judy?"

"I don't think so." As I climbed into my car, the crowd of onlookers disbursed. I felt like a limp dishrag. As I pulled away, Jessica waved at me. When

I lifted my arm to wave back, it felt like it weighed a ton.

CHAPTER FIFTEEN

A Tangled Web

On a balmy evening in May, I attended a party at Connie's apartment, a spacious and luxurious place with a breathtaking view of the mountains. It was her 10th AA "Birthday", a real milestone, and at least 15 friends from AA were celebrating with us, laughing and dancing to Sting's "Every Breath You Take". I was so proud of Connie; she had followed her dream of working in the holistic health field and, after struggling for several years, going to school part time while still working at her high-powered, demanding sales job, she was officially ready to open her own massage practice. Watching everyone congratulate Connie, I had to admit to myself I felt a little melancholy, wondering if I would ever achieve my own goal of having my writing published. And I was angry at myself for letting Jessica become a constant interference on my energy; my writing had suffered tremendously. Not only that, but I had also gained six pounds in the past few months, just from eating during the night when I couldn't sleep. I blamed that on Jessica too. There was a huge table of food in

Connie's dining room and I had to force myself to take some salad and a diet soda when I really wanted to fill my plate with barbequed ribs and a buttery ear of corn! I found a comfortable seat on the sofa and told myself to forget Jessica and just have some fun. I looked around and smiled as I watched my friends enjoying themselves. Since everyone present was a recovering alcoholic/addict, there was no alcohol being served but the party was still lively and boisterous. I was just about to start eating when suddenly there was a loud uproar.

"Quiet everybody! Turn off the music!" yelled Jeff, a young man with dreadlocks and an earring. The room quieted down and Jeff turned up the volume on the big-screen TV in the living room. I pushed my way through the crowd so I could see what was going on. The image before me was one I would never forget; there was Jessica Wilson, wearing a frumpy blue jail uniform, standing in front of a judge in a crowded courtroom. Her wrists and ankles were shackled and her hair was a mess; she looked like someone you might see roaming the streets, poking through garbage cans. In spite of myself I felt sorry for her. A well-dressed man in his late 30s was speaking into a microphone from outside the courtroom.

"Yesterday the Grand Jury unsealed an indictment charging 45-yearold Jessica Wilson with first-degree murder in the shooting death of her ex-husband, Nicholas Wilson in her home on February 7th,, 1992.

Judge Sandra McSorley issued a warrant for Mrs. Wilson's arrest. Wilson turned herself in last night at 7:00 p.m. at the Scottsdale County Stockade." A photo of Jessica's house appeared on the screen. The partiers yelled as if their football team had just made a touchdown.

"She's goin' down!" Jeff yelled.

"She's gonna fry!" someone else yelled. Connie came over and put her arm around me. She had kind blue eyes and a mellow aura that was always comforting.

"Are you okay sweetie?" Her voice was calm and soothing. I shook my head.

"I don't know. I mean, I can't say I'm surprised but it's all so bizarre!" Connie nodded and hugged me and we turned our attention back to the TV.

"Jessica Wilson pleaded innocent to the charges. She is being held at the Scottsdale County Stockade without bail. To keep her in jail, prosecutors called firearms expert John O'Rourke from the Sheriff's office to testify that all three shots from the .357 Magnum were fired from four to six feet away. Forensic expert Bruce Dahlson says that Nicholas Wilson could not have had a knife in his hand because gunpowder found on the palms of his hands indicates that during the firing of the shots, his hands were in an open, exposed position. Mr. Dahlson testified that he believes the knife would likely have been placed in Mr. Wilson's hands after the shooting occurred. The shooting is a culmination of a divorce that escalated out of control. Tragically, just seven hours before he was killed, Nicholas Wilson had persuaded the Circuit Judge to grant a psychological evaluation of his ex-wife, claiming her behavior was unstable and irrational. It was the third time he had asked for this evaluation. To corroborate his charges of mental instability, Wilson had quoted the lawsuit of Joshua Swenson, an attorney who had dated Mrs. Wilson. When Swenson ended the relationship, she slashed his tires, made harassing phone calls to him and his friends and climbed up a ladder to his outdoor porch and turned on the propane valve of his gas grill. A judge issued Swenson a restraining order against Jessica Wilson."

"Jesus!" yelled Jeff. "That's the first I've heard of that. She's nuttier than a fruitcake!"

I swallowed hard, feeling like I was choking.

The newscaster went on. "Nicholas Wilson had also remarked that same day to the judge that he didn't understand the intensity of Jessica Wilson's anger; that it reminded him of a "Fatal Attraction" situation. He informed the judge that Jessica often left the boys alone to pursue "overnight liaisons with companions" and said that she had refused to let him visit the boys since Thanksgiving. Mr. Wilson's attorney, said they were very relieved about the ruling from Judge Hoy. According to the court order, Mr. Wilson would have custody of the boys on alternate weekends, the first weekend would have begun at 5 p.m. Friday February 7th, the exact day and time he was killed. At 4:30 p.m. Dennison called Nicholas Wilson at his office; Wilson dreaded another confrontation with Jessica but Dennison encouraged him to try to get his boys, even if Jessica refused, because it was important to exercise his visitation rights. Neither of the men believed Nicholas would wind up with the children that night, according to Dennison. Tragically, that was correct. The judge never even had a chance to sign the order.

Gabriel Meyers, Jessica's attorney, appeared on the screen, looking very smug. "We have filed a motion for a bond hearing, which has been set for April 28th. The shooting around which this case revolves was an act of self-defense."

The newscaster went on to say that Jessica told the circuit court judge that she had only $25.26 in her checking account and lacked the income to pay a lawyer. She said she is unemployed and last worked as a limousine driver. The Public Defender's Office declined to handle the case because John McDonald, senior trial officer in its' capital division, is friends with the Wilson family.

"She's broke and she gets Meyers! That figures. Meyers is supposed to be a really good criminal attorney. He hardly ever loses a case!" one of the partiers commented.

We turned our attention back to the news. "Her children are staying with a friend," the man went on.

"What friend?" somebody yelled. "She doesn't have any friends!"

"Those poor kids," Connie said quietly.

"I know," I sighed. "I tried to help them . . ."

She hugged me. "Sweetie, you did way more than most people would have. You just have to let it go." The TV was turned off and everyone at the party continued to discuss the case. Most were convinced that Jessica had committed a pre-meditated murder. We were all filled with righteous indignation. After a while, it started feeling like a lynch mob.

Connie suggested we all "mellow out" and the discussion got more spiritual. We realized we were judging her, something we were taught not to do in AA. We had an impromptu meeting and ended up joining hands and saying "The Lord's Prayer" and "The Serenity Prayer". Connie offered to give me a massage and she went out to her car and got her portable massage table and brought it in and set it up in the bedroom. I was so tense I felt sick to my stomach. Connie put on some quiet new-age music and began kneading my aching neck muscles. Little by little, I began relaxing. As I drifted off into a dream-like state, I wondered again what had happened to Jessica in her childhood to make her the way she was. I remembered she had told me her mother was "crazy" and at the time I had thought she was exaggerating but now I wondered; maybe Jessica had inherited manic-depression or some other genetic mental illness. I wondered, too, just when, or if, this drama with her would ever end. It seemed she was my cross to bear.

CHAPTER SIXTEEN

The Facts

After "the arrest", I gave up trying to detach from the whole situation. In the days and weeks after Jessica's arrest, the newspaper was constantly full of articles about her case. I couldn't help myself; I devoured them. I admit I was fascinated. I mean, how often did these things happen to someone I knew? My life had been relatively mundane before this. Much of what I heard and read about Jessica and Nicholas I already knew but some was new information and it filled in the blanks for me. There had always been so much I had wondered about and I never really knew if she was telling me the truth about anything. Now I had all the facts being presented to me in black and white!

I wasn't at all surprised to read that the file folder that Nicholas had used to carry his missing will and more than $1 million in life insurance policies were found in Jessica's house. Nicholas's family had been trying to untangle the "mystery" of the will's whereabouts and Rosemary Wilson suggested to the sheriff to check Jessica's residence, which had been sitting empty since she killed Nicholas. Without the will, the boys would have inherited Nicholas's estate right away instead of when they were 35 and Jessica would have become guardian of the estate. But since Rosemary and Michael Wilson came forward and verified the contents of the will, it was reinstated. The only mystery to me was that they didn't look in Jessica's house right away!

After Jessica sued Nicholas for back alimony and child support, his estate then sued Jessica, filing a civil lawsuit claiming that she shot him "without any justification or reasonable cause." An attorney for the First National Bank in Scottdale filed the suit in response to Jessica's lawsuit. There was a big story about Jessica's "strained relationship" with the Wilson family which grew worse in the months after she and Nicholas were divorced. Doug Wilson wrote in a letter to the court that Jessica "staged an appearance . . . mocking their grief" at their father's funeral when she wore the white mini-dress. The letter went on to say, "tales of her rage include references to handguns, assaults, trespass, vandalism, slander, public profanity and uncontrollable hysteria. Door locks have been changed to protect us from Jessica, telephone numbers have been changed. We cannot afford to take her malicious threats lightly." This led me to believe that she already knew how to use a gun, which she had never mentioned to me. I could certainly relate to changing telephone numbers when I thought of all the times I tried to get her to stop calling me. I read that, when Nicholas's sisters would call to speak to the boys, the boys would say "I can't talk to you. My mom said you're a slut." Jessica also told the boys that their uncles were "preoccupied with sex". None of this surprised me at all; Jessica's hatred for the family was something she never tried to hide.

The paper mentioned that when Nicholas's father died in 1988, he divided $1.5 million of his estate into 8 shares. Six of the siblings each received a share, Rosemary Wilson got two and Nicholas got nothing. I remembered that Jessica had been enraged about this at Mr. Wilson's funeral. The article also mentioned a Wilson party during which Jessica had interrupted and the phone call to Susie Wilson I'd overheard that day at her house, when she'd screamed, "You're going to pay for this Susie! Your family is going to pay and your brother is going to pay!" Assistant State Prosecuting Attorney Peter Hart asked Circuit Court Judge Chang to set bail at $200,000 because he said the killing was a "planned, premeditated killing for money and so that the deceased could not gain custody of the wo children." However, after hearing two days of testimony, the judge ruled that Jessica was entitled to bail while she awaits the trial and he set the bail at $75,000. When she was released, he instructed her not to discuss the case with the boys.

Prosecutor Hart may call the boys as witnesses in the case and he is "very concerned" that Jessica will discuss the case with them. "I think any normal person, whether they are a prosecutor or not, would be worried about it," he said. "How is the judge's order going to be enforceable?"

Valerie Henning, a court appointed guardian ad litem for the boys, agreed with Judge Chang. She stated "They really need her at this time." Stan Johlson, an investigator with the State Department of Health and Rehabilitation also agreed, saying "It's been devastating for them. They believe that the sun and moon rise with their mother. She is the most important person in their lives." The story said that Jessica and the boys were staying with someone named Sherry, who had even promised Jessica a job upon her release. Knowing Jessica as I did, I figured she wasn't really interested in working and would milk Nicholas's estate for everything she could get.

I wasn't surprised to read that the arrangement baffled the friends and family of Nicholas. "To recommend that these two children be placed in the hands of their father's killer makes a Stephen King novel appear tame!" said Elizabeth Stevens, Nicholas Wilson's ex-roommate, in a letter written in self-defense. Prosecutor Hart would not comment on the judge's order releasing Jessica and simply remarked, "All I can say is, the prosecution will go forward."

I was getting tired and upset as I read all the stories about Jessica. I made myself a cup of hot cocoa and took a hot bath. I tried to go to sleep but my mind was so over-stimulated by all that I had been absorbing about her, I gave up and turned on my reading lamp and grabbed the newspapers again.

There was a picture of Jessica's Attorney, Gabriel Meyers, in an article. I had heard stories about him; he was called the "Champion of the underdog", described as a "Woodstock Nation refugee" who wore his hair in an Afro in the sixties and defended the poor. Now his clients were rich and he wore Armani suits. He was a familiar figure around Scottsdale n his turquoise Harley bike, smoking a fat cigar. Meyers cemented his reputation in a murder-for-hire case when he bombarded a government snitch with so much evidence, the man capitulated.

Meyers described Nicholas Wilson as a man who seemed quiet and calm to others but '"turned violent behind closed doors." Police were called to the Wilson home four times in 1983 for "domestic violence". At that time they lived in a patio home and were friends with many attorneys, including the prosecutor in the William Kennedy Smith trial, who was a neighbor of the Wilsons.

According to Jessica, Nicholas beat her and put her in the hospital several times. Later however, she dropped the charges. Police reports dating back to 1983 support the claims. On October 11, 1987, Jessica took the boys to a nearby fire station after an argument over money turned violent.he told paramedics Nicholas had beaten her for years and that he said he would kill her if she divorced him. That didn't make sense to me since Nicholas had WANTED a divorce!

Atty. Meyers was quoted as saying, "There is ample evidence
that this was a very violent and abusive man, the post-mortem praise notwithstanding. It is not a crime to kill somebody who you fear is going to kill you." He also stated, "There won't be an issue as to whether he used to beat her." However, Nicholas Wilson's divorce attorney, Robert Dennison, believes it will be "tremendously difficult" for Jessica to claim abuse as an excuse for the killing. "She hadn't lived with Nicholas for four years and she never went to divorce court complaining about that and never sought an injunction," he said.

A judge postponed ruling on whether the Wilson brothers should testify at Jessica's trial.

And it was decided that if they did testify, it would be in the judge's chambers rather than a crowded courtroom. The jury would be able to watch the boys' testimony via a closed-circuit television.

Jessica also told a judge that Nicholas forgot the boys' birthdays and sometimes left them with relatives and sent them home in a taxi. She claimed in divorce papers that the problems started in 1987 when Nicholas began seeing another woman. I didn't know what to believe. I knew Nicholas had had an affair, but I wondered. . . if he really had been beating her all those years, why did she stay with him, even if he had a lot of money? And did she make him crazy enough to beat her? I'd felt like smacking her a few times myself! Jessica told police that Nicholas had been under investigation for money-laundering charges and said he only visited the boys sporadically. She also claimed that Nicholas abandoned the boys in a hotel room, beat them and told them they were worthless. This didn't ring true to me because in all the time I'd spent with her, she'd never mentioned any of this. And the boys always seemed happy when they were going to spend time with Nicholas. Jessica also said Nicholas used support payments as a means to have her beg him for money. It was hard for me to sort out exactly how I felt when I read all these things but I recalled the day Nicholas had generously given her money for Art Fest. The more I read, the more I felt that Jessica was guilty of pre-meditated murder. But would the jury think so?

CHAPTER SEVENTEEN

Back and Blue

A week after Connie's party, I was still upset so I went shopping at the local mall for some retail therapy. I left my car at Sears Automotive Center to have it tuned up while I browsed through the stores. The midway was crowded and I contemplated going to the dusty, dismal waiting room at Sears and just sitting. My Chronic Fatigue was really kicking in from the constant stress of emotional ups and downs related to Jessica. But I said a quick prayer and one of my favorite AA slogans "move a muscle, change a thought" came to mind and I decided to keep going. A chocolate protein drink from the health food store gave me a burst of energy and I kept walking, looking in store windows listening to "Do You Believe in Magic" on the loudspeakers.

The song always brought to mind good times, hopeful times, my sophomore year at high school when I blossomed from a dorky, too tall, ne-skinned 14 year old into a pretty girl with waist length hair and clear skin, thanks to my parents who managed to find the money for a dermatologist. All of a sudden I had more boyfriends than I knew what to do with. I thought about Trevor, wondering what his teenage years would be like. Impulsively I decided to buy myself a beautiful yellow and black hairclip in the shape of a butterfly that had caught my attention. As I paid for it, I had a flash back to when I first met Jessica and had compared her to a beautiful butterfly that had been battered down and bruised. I sighed; a deep sadness came over me. I fervently wished things had turned out differently, wished Jayson and Brian Wilson still had a father. I found myself at Lord and Taylors, checking out the sale rack in the upscale women's clothing section. I was approached by a slender, attractive saleswoman wearing a smart beige linen outfit. Her brown eyes were warm and her auburn hair was short and stylish. Her nametag read "Nancy."

"Can I help you?" She said in a friendly voice.

"Oh, thank you. I'm looking for something nice for work. A suit perhaps . . . or a coat dress."

"We have some new items here by Ann Taylor that would look stunning on you."

"Well I really can't afford anything full price. Maybe something on sale?"

"Of course. You're so tall and have such a lovely figure. Have you ever done any modeling?"

"A little, here and there. Just a few fashion shows locally." It was a nice compliment since I felt "fat" right now. I flashed back to when I was 18 and had moved to Chicago to attend modeling school. But instead of finishing school, I had gotten strung out on speed, trying to be skinny enough. I had befriended a raven-haired woman named Anna who only dated black men. She took me to a party in a gorgeous mansion in the suburbs where Billy Preston and his band were among the guests. I ended up spending a wild weekend doing coke with Billy and the band!

Nancy shook her head. "You remind me so much of Jessica Wilson. Do you know her?"

"Yes, I'm acquainted with her." I groaned inwardly. Shit!

"You're both so beautiful. I can't get over the resemblance! You are probably the same size; in fact that dress you're wearing looks like something she would have bought." Nancy looked around to make sure no one was listening, then stepped closer to me and talked softly. "I feel so sorry for that poor girl. That ex-husband of hers put her through hell!" I assumed Nancy had read about the Wilsons in the paper. I sighed. Maybe I should consider moving to Alaska or Mexico. If Jessica did somehow walk away a free woman, I'd never escape this constant comparison to her.

"I got to know her well," Nancy went on. "When she shopped here, she always made an appointment with me in advance, to wait on her. She almost always had bruises on her neck and back! And she had to wear sunglasses to hide the bruises around her eyes!"

"When was this Nancy? Recently?" It felt like a corkscrew was turning inside my stomach.

"On and off for the past few years."

I knew that Jessica and Nicholas supposedly had violent fights in the early 1980s, but they had been divorced for several years before she killed him, and she hadn't mentioned a word about any physical abuse since I'd met her.

"Nancy, it must have been a while ago, right? I mean, she hasn't been in here recently with bruises, has she?"

"Well, let's see . . . yes . . . recently she came in to buy clothes to wear to court, to her divorce proceedings."

I felt frustrated and confused, thrown off track. This information didn't fit into my vast puzzle of knowledge of "all things Jessica ". When I had "spied" on her and Nicholas that day at the Courthouse last year, she was wearing old, shabby clothes. Nancy went on. "She always worried so about spending too much money, even though Nicholas wore shirts that were custom-made in Palm Beach!"

This, too, didn't ring true for me. Jessica usually seemed to give herself free rein when buying clothes.

"We became friends," Nancy continued. "I wanted to invite her to my home, to dinner, but I was afraid to get involved. She told me her brotherin-law put out a contract on her and she was terrified!"

I felt like the wind had been knocked out of me. It was one thing to read about Jessica saying Nicholas had beat her, but quite another to hear that someone had witnessed bruises on her body! I wondered again if I had been wrong about Jessica. I felt like I was back at square one!

"She called me and asked if I would testify for her in court, about the bruises. But I was afraid to get involved. She even called again this morning as a matter of fact! Can you imagine?"

"She did?" I was again glad I had changed my number.

"I'm going up North in a week, and besides, I have heart trouble. I couldn't take the stress, you know. I felt bad but I had to say so. I guess I'm a coward."

I squeezed Nancy's hand. "You're not a coward! Jessica is lucky to have a friend like you."

I was too distracted to make a decision to purchase anything so I left, promising Nancy I would be back soon. She gave me her card. I picked up my car at Sears, feeling spacey and rattled. Behind the wheel, I was concentrating so hard on processing what I just heard that I almost got in an accident, stopping at the very last minute at a stop sign! The driver coming the other way honked his horn and shook his fist at me. I felt a mounting sense of desperation and for some reason I found myself driving by Jessica's empty home. There was still orange police tape across the front door, windows and garage. The yard was unkempt, a window was broken; the once beautiful house stood, sad and empty, like an old person waiting to die.

Later that night I called Freddie and told him what Nancy had shared with me.

"Judy, I don't believe a word of it. She's capable of faking her own bruises. People do it all the time. It's not that hard; I've represented women who did it and they weren't half as crazy as Jessica ! Judy, she's a sociopath! She has no conscious, no scruples, she'll stop at nothing. She's very devious. Don't get sucked back in feeling sorry for her."

"Yeah, you're right Freddie. It just didn't make sense . . ."

"You watch, she'll try to force that poor woman to testify for her. She was setting her up. That's how she operates."

"I should call Nancy and warn her."

"I think you should.

CHAPTER EIGHTEEN

The Circus

It was May 11, 1993, over a year after the shooting, when Jessica's FirstDegree Murder case finally went to court. I had invested in a more flattering wig and I wore it every time I went out. It was impossible not to hear about the case. Even the supermarket tabloids boasted articles with headlines like "Scottsdale Socialite Murders Ex-Husband! Was it really self- defense?" Jessica's picture was everywhere. The story made front-page news every day. I read that 73 prospective jurors answered a barrage of questions from attorneys, including queries about their favorite television shows, marital status and whether they had ever had a gun pointed at them. They were also asked if they were color blind, if they had ever wanted to be a police officer and what the term "self-defense" meant to them. According to the papers, Jessica conferred with her attorneys and smiled politely to jurors as they left the courtroom. Jessica had told a 911 operator that she killed her husband in self-defense after he came at her with a knife. The prosecutor said he would prove that Jessica Wilson planted a knife in Nicholas's hand after she shot him. Circuit Court Judge James Van Buren would be presiding over the trial.

According to the papers, shortly before she shot Nicholas, Jessica illegally taped a phone call in which she asked about the status of his life insurance policy, her attorney admitted. Meyers made the odd admission in an effort to bar the jury from hearing the tape. Arizona law prohibits juries from hearing evidence that is obtained illegally and Nicholas Wilson did not know he was being recorded. On the tape, they argued. He accused her of spending too much money. She repeatedly asked him to meet her on Friday.

Later in the conversation she asked, "Where's the life insurance? Do you still have life insurance?"

"Yes," Nicholas replied.

"Who's the beneficiary?"

"You are."

"I don't want to be the beneficiary. The children better be!"

Circuit Judge Van Buren said he would decide whether the jury should hear the tape. As Jayson Wilson called 911 that day, seven dial tones could be heard in the background. Then Jessica's voice was heard, crying hysterically. She had been trying to call Jimmy Fischer, a friend and attorney. Prosecutor Peter Hart argued "If she was so traumatized by a self-defense shooting, she would have called 911 first, not someone else."

After a lot of soul searching, I finally decided I did want to attend the trial, if for no other reason than that I was just plain curious! Plus, I hoped it would give me some kind of closure or peace about the situation. I was even willing to use some of my precious vacation time from work to be there. As I pulled into the parking lot, there were dozens of people huddled on the courthouse steps swarming around like vultures. Several police cars parked near the entrance. A large area was cordoned off as if a rock star was appearing! I had my wig on and wore horn-rimmed glasses. My bailiff friend Johnny had promised to try and save me a good seat. I pushed my way through the crowd and after flashing my fake press ID to a policeman, a security guard waved a metal detector in front of me. Finally I made it through the door. When I finally got to the courtroom, it was packed. I saw Johnny and he motioned for me to follow him. He led me to an empty seat right up at the front of the room in the press section! I sat down, waiting for the performance to begin. I took out a pad of paper and a pen and pretended to be taking notes. There were quite a few cameras at the back of the room and people from Court TV were there. Jessica had dyed her hair a soft auburn and wore barrettes and no jewelry. She was dressed in a demure beige dress that was longer than dresses she usually wore. The Wilson siblings sat in the front row with grim expressions.

Prosecutor Hart plunged right into the case, starting with the recording of the voice of Jessica as Jayson called 911 right after his father was shot.

"Jessica Wilson's voice reveals an incriminating emotional control when she unexpectantly found herself talking to police just moments after shooting and killing her former husband. She was trying to call Jimmy Fischer, a friend who was an attorney. She didn't realize that her son was already on the extension with the police." Hart looked at the jurors. "I'll ask you to pay particular attention to the tone of her voice, to how her voice changed from an argumentative," Who is this?" to immediately becoming hysterical, saying "Nicholas Wilson was coming up the hallway towards me with a knife and I shot him." Nicholas Wilson, 42, was shot in the left front shoulder, under the right arm and in the back of the head."

Defense Atty. Gabriel Meyers countered that the case against Jessica Wilson is a product of "gross negligence, incompetent investigations and assumptions based on facts that don't exist." He asked jurors to note the real distress in her voice on the 911 tape, which was played several times in the courtroom. "She was hysterical and you can hear it!" he said, as Jessica wept quietly at the defense table. "You'll hear she fired those shots as Nicholas Wilson stood there confronting her with a knife in his hands." Meyers also noted the depth of Nicholas Wilson's hostility towards his ex-wife, saying Nicholas once told her, during a debate over life insurance, "If you were dead, I could chop you up and make fertilizer out of you!"

Hart interjected, "The blood splatter evidence will prove the shot to Nicholas Wilson's head was fired from about a foot away after he had fallen to the floor. He could not have been holding a knife when he was shot."

Meyers refuted this, saying that Nicholas was shot three times while standing.

The re-enactment of the shooting was shown. Jurors perched on the edge of their chairs, family members covered their mouths and Jessica looked away as an expert witness used a mannequin dressed in Nicholas Wilson's bloody clothing. The crowded courtroom hushed as Rod Englert, a crime scene reconstruction expert hired by the prosecution, pierced the foam rubber mannequin with long knitting needles to show the paths of the three bullets. According to Englert, the first shot hit Wilson in the left shoulder and spun him to his left. The bullet went through him and broke a window pane in a French door behind him. His arms were raised and his hands were open. The second shot hit Wilson under his right arm as he fell to the ground. His left leg buckled under him and he fell onto his left side and stomach. The third shot, fired from within 15 inches, hit him in the back of the head as he lay on the floor. Under Englert's scenario, Nicholas was then rolled onto his back. Urine stains on his pants indicate that he was lying on his left side and his gold necklace had fallen toward his left shoulder. His hair brushed against a blood splatter on a nearby table when he was rolled onto his back.

"Do you have an opinion on how the knife got into his hand?" Hart asked.

"It was placed in his right hand," Englert said.

"By himself or another person?"

"By Mrs. Wilson," Englert replied.

Jessica's attorney jumped to his feet and asked for a mistrial. Circuit Judge Van Buren told the jurors to disregard Englert's answer and warned Englert against commenting on Jessica Wilson's guilt or innocence.

During cross examination, Englert, a police officer in Oregon, said he has rarely testified for the defense during 30 years of working as a reconstruction expert. He is paid $150 an hour and has put more than 200 hours on the Wilson case. He admitted Wilson's necklace could have been moved when paramedics ripped open his shirt.

The crowded courtroom was cleared and the judge barred the public and only one reporter was allowed in the courtroom during testimony from 8-year-old Jayson Wilson. I was able to sit in another room where his testimony was shown on a closed-circuit television. Jessica looked proudly at her son as he walked timidly up to the witness chair. Prosecutor Hart positioned himself beside the jury box so that Jayson would not have to look at his mother as he answered questions. Meyers, however, stood so that Jayson would have to look at his mother during cross examination.

The gangly, freckle-faced, red-haired boy clutched a small, red plastic super-hero for support and spoke softly during two hours of testimony as he described the shots his mother fired from a .357 Magnum while he watched from a crack in the bedroom door.

"It happened so fast," Jayson said. "It was so loud my ears were ringing and the flash of light kind of made everything go red." Jayson gave his mother a quick smile but rarely looked at her during testimony. Hart squatted to Jayson's level as he questioned him.

"Jayson, I know this is difficult. Just do your best, tell the truth. That's all you have to do."

Jayson nodded solemnly. "I really want to help my mom."

"Of course you do Jayson. Just tell us, in your own words what happened the night of Feb. 7, 1992."

"Okay. Well, me and my brother were waiting for Dad to come over. I heard his car pull into the driveway at about 5:00 p.m. He stayed in the car for a while. Mom told her us to go to our bedroom and pack our bags. A few minutes later, I heard a loud slam and I asked Mom if she was okay. When she didn't answer, I peered out the bedroom door and saw my dad walking down the hallway. My mom was scrunched against the wall, holding something that I later realized was a gun. Dad said something like "What is this?" Then I saw Mom shoot my dad. I slammed the door shut after the second shot but, because the door had no doorknob on it, it didn't stay shut. I looked out again and saw my dad lying in the hallway. I saw something in his hand, that's the first thing I saw when I opened the door," Jayson said. "It had a glary shine." Police found a knife with an 8 ½ in blade in Nicholas Wilson's right hand and his car keys were between his legs.

But, during cross examination by Defense Atty. Meyers, Jayson offered a slightly different version. Meyers asked Jayson again to tell the jurors what happened.

"Well, I think my dad came into the house and told Mom that he had a court order allowing him to visit me and my brother. I heard Mom scream, "No!"

Meyers asked Jayson, "Did your dad say "This is it'?""

"It sounded like that, I think," Jayson replied, appearing somewhat doubtful.

"What happened then Jayson?"

"I saw my mom shoot my dad. I ran to the phone and dialed 911. I heard my mom on the extension phone dialing a number. I guess she didn't realize that I was already on the line with the police. She punched in seven numbers and began saying, "Jimmy, Jimmy, pick up!"

(Detectives later learned that the number she had called was Scottsdale real estate attorney James Fischer, a friend of Jessica Wilson.) I told the dispatcher, "Help, there's been a shooting!"

"Mom's voice then came on the line and she said "Is this the police?" When the dispatcher said it was, she then began crying hysterically, saying her ex-husband had just tried to kill her. Then she hung up. The 911 operator re-dialed the number several times and let it ring a bunch of times before Mom finally answered again. This time she was even more hysterical. My mom came into the bedroom with me and my brother, who was hiding in a closet. Then she got down on the floor on her back and braced the door shut with her feet."

"Jayson, can you show us what that looked like?" Meyers said.

"Sure". Jayson got down from the witness chair and lay down on the floor to demonstrate to the jury how Jessica did this. He leaned against the podium and pushed his legs out as if bracing himself against a door. Jayson told the jurors that soon the police arrived and took the family to the Scottsdale Police Department. Jessica Wilson declined to give a statement and became hysterical. Paramedics who examined her said her pulse was only "mildly raised", prompting them to question if her "vital signs coincided with the level of distress she was portraying to us," Scottsdale Police Detective Jay Ramariz wrote in his report.

A courtroom examination of the bloody shirt and sweater worn by Nicholas Wilson when he was found dead brought gasps of horror from his family and tears to the eyes of his ex-wife. Jessica turned her head away and stared down at the floor when Assistant State Atty. Hart removed a bloody, blue sweater from an evidence bag for a firearm expert to examine. Nicholas Wilson's brothers and sisters, who filled the first two rows of the courtroom, were visibly moved when Hart showed the jury the once white shirt that their brother had worn, now covered with dried blood. Jessica covered her mouth and stifled sobs as John O'Rourke, a firearms expert at the Scottsdale County Sheriff's Office, poked his gloved fingers through two bullet holes in the shirt. O'Rourke said he test-fired the .357 caliber revolver used in the shooting dozens of times at various distances from a target. After studying gunpowder left on Nicholas Wilson's clothing, he determined that two of the shots were fired from four to six feet away. The shot behind Nicholas's right ear was fired from 9 to 15 inches away.

However, during cross-examination by Gabriel Meyers, O'Rourke admitted he had failed to bring the equipment he needed to perform the crucial tests when he was called to Jessica Wilson's home at about

1:00 a.m. on Feb. 8, 1992. Although he stopped by the Sheriff's office lab on his way to the investigation, O'Rourke couldn't find any string, which is used to study the trajectory of a bullet. He said he stopped at several convenience stores but none sold string. Flustered, O'Rourke also admitted that he didn't bring the chemicals needed to determine if a bullet ricocheted off a two-by-four in Jessica Wilson's kitchen. Instead of cutting out the suspected ricochet dent and taking it to his lab, he tried to conduct the test using vinegar, tap water, gauze and Jessica Wilson's iron. The faces of the Wilson family looked angry at hearing this. Jessica tried to hide a smile. I knew the mistakes he had made would cost the prosecution a lot. At this point everyone was exhausted and Judge Van Buren called for a recess until the following day. I was very relieved; I was emotionally drained.

Saturday morning I slept late, still exhausted from the courtroom drama. I poured some coffee and sat down to read the paper while Trevor watched cartoons. A picture of Jessica stared back at me from the front page of the paper. I read the article below it.

JUDGE IS REPLACED IN WILSON CASE

Veteran criminal Court Judge Carl Harper was substituted Friday to preside over next week's Jessica Wilson murder trial after Wilson's attorney asked that

Circuit Court Judge Chang step aside. Chang was removed after attorney Melissa Gamot was overheard in a courthouse hallway telling Chang that she hoped he had an opportunity to "burn the defendant". Sara Blumer, the attorney who overheard Gamot's comment reported to Chief Judge Jack Cook, who in turn asked Chang to review whether he might be prejudiced against Wilson. Chang said that he could still be fair. "I don't attach any great significance to it," he said of the remark. "It does not affect me any more than reading a newspaper account of pending criminal charges would." But Chang asked Gabriel Meyers, Jessica Wilson's attorney, to review the situation. Meyers formally asked on Friday that Chang step aside.

I had to laugh; I knew a lot of people who agreed with Melina Gamot! Jessica's reputation in Scottsdale was legendary!

The next day I barely managed to get a seat in the packed courtroom. It was even more crowded than it had been the day before. Again, Nicholas's siblings filled the two whole rows behind Hart. His first witness was Dr. John Wiewora, who had performed the autopsy on Nicholas. I braced myself for the gory details and hoped I wouldn't get sick.

"Please state your name, sir, for the Court."

"Dr. John Wiewora."

"And please tell us what your specialty is."

"I am a medical examiner."

"And did you perform the autopsy on Nicholas Wilson?"

"I did."

"And how many times was he shot?"

"Three times."

"From what type of gun?"

"From a .357 Magnum."

Hart turned at this point and faced the room. "I would like to introduce into the evidence photographs of the back of Nicholas Wilson's head which were taken after he was killed." He passed some photographs to the jurors. One by one, the jurors looked with absolute horror at the pictures. Jessica sobbed and she dropped her head on Meyers' shoulders. There was quiet in the room for a few minutes as the photographs were examined. Jessica's crying became louder; she acted like she was going to have a breakdown.

The Judge pounded his gavel. "Court will be recessed for 15 minutes so that Mrs. Wilson can compose herself." Jessica was escorted from the room with the help of Meyers while the Wilson family members watched her with animosity. When she was almost to the door, she appeared to faint and Meyers grabbed her and held her up.

Bravo, I felt like shouting. Jessica, you really should have been an actress!

When Court was resumed, Dr. Wiewora took the stand again. Hart stood right in front of him as he was questioned. "What did you find when you examined Nicholas Wilson's hand?"

"I found gunpowder on the palms of his hands."

"What did the gunpowder indicate to you Dr.Wiewora?"

"It indicated that Nicholas Wilson's hands were open when he was shot."

"Do you feel that he could have been holding a knife when he was shot?"

"No, I do not."

"Where did the shots enter Mr. Wilson's body?"

"Two of the shots hit him from the right read side, one in the back of the neck and the other just below his right armpit. The third shot, to the neck, left gunpowder on the side of his neck and face. His right arm would have had to have been raised for him to have been shot beneath his right armpit."

"Again, sir, it is your belief that Nicholas Wilson was not holding a knife when he was shot?"

"Yes, it is. I do not believe he could have been holding a knife."

"Thank you, Doctor. No further questions."

Meyers declined to cross-examine and the doctor was excused. Meyers called to the witness stand Dr. Herbert Barns. He was in his 50s, a stocky man with a goatee and dark hair. I had never heard Jessica mention him.

After Barnes was sworn in, Meyers began questioning him.

"Please state your name for the Court sir."

"Dr. Herbert Barnes."

"What field of medicine do you specialize in?"

"I am a psychotherapist."

"Where do you practice?"

"In Scottsdale."

"How do you know the defendant?"

"I've known Jessica Wilson socially for about five years."

"Dr. Barnes, did you speak to Mrs. Wilson on February 7, 1992?"

"I did."

"Approximately what time did you speak to her?"

"It was about 3:15 p.m."

"How long did you talk?"

"Oh . . . probably about two hours."

"What state of mind did Mrs. Wilson seem to be in that afternoon?"

"She seemed normal and friendly."

"Did she mention what she had done that day?"

"Yes. She said that she had gone grocery shopping at Safeway and had taken her boys to get haircuts."

"Did you have any reason to believe Mrs. Wilson was upset about anything that day?"

"No, none at all. She was quite pleasant and seemed calm."

"Thank you Doctor. No further questions."

Hart declined to cross examine and Dr. Barnes was dismissed. I wondered how Jessica could be friends with a psychotherapist and be so damn crazy! And his testimony didn't change my mind at all. I knew how cunning and devious Jessica could be. I wouldn't put it past her to have called him just to help her establish her alibi!

The next witness was Jimmy Fischer, the real estate lawyer Jessica had called right after she shot Nicholas. He was an attractive man with blond hair. I wondered if Jessica had been romantically involved with him. He was sworn in.

"Please state your name sir." Meyers said.

"James Fischer."

"What is your profession?"

"I'm a real estate attorney in Phoenix."

"What is your relationship with the defendant?"

"We've been friends for about eight years."

"Did you and Mrs. Wilson have plans to see each other the night Nicholas Wilson was killed?"

"Yes, we did. We were going to take our kids out to dinner and a movie that night."

"Did Jessica Wilson call you that night?"

"Yes. She called me about 5:30 p.m."

"What did she say?"

"She said that Nicholas Wilson had tried to kill her with a knife and she shot him."

"What state of mind was she in, in your opinion?"

"She was hysterical."

"Did you go to her house then?"

"I met her and the boys at the Scottsdale Police Station."

"Are you Mrs. Wilson's attorney?"

"No. I did some real estate work for her a few years back. But we're just friends. Not romantically involved, just friends. Our kids play with each other."

"When was the next time you saw Mrs. Wilson after the shooting?"

"The next morning. I went to her house."

"Was there anything you noticed in the house? Anything unusual?"

"Well, she had left her groceries out, unpacked, on the counter. All the milk and frozen foods were sitting out, getting warm and melting, as if she had been interrupted before she could put them away."

"Thank you Mr. Fischer. No further questions."

Hart declined to cross examine James Fischer and he was dismissed. Hart then called Nicholas's lawyer, Robert Dennison, to the stand. He was probably in his mid-50s and was bald and wore thick glasses. He was sworn in.

"Please state your name for the Court." Hart said.

"Robert Dennison."

"What is your profession?"

"I'm an attorney. In Scottsdale."

"Was Nicholas Wilson a client of yours?"

"Yes. I represented him for about 10 years."

"Did you speak to Mr. Wilson the week he was killed?"

"Yes, about three days before he was killed."

"What did you talk about?"

"He told me that Jessica Wilson had called him to discuss the disposition of the house she was living in."

"What did she say?"

"She got very angry and the gist of what she said to him was, "If you were dead, at least the life insurance would pay off the mortgage."

"Did you see Nicholas Wilson after that?"

"Yes, we were in Court the morning he was shot. He had been granted custody of the boys. He was relieved, but also worried about what Jessica would do when he went to pick them up."

"Mr. Dennison, when were you notified that Nicholas Wilson had been killed?"

"The police called me around 6:00 p.m. that day."

"Thank you sir. No further questions."

Meyers declined to cross examine Dennison and Mr. Dennison stepped down from the witness stand. Next Meyers called Gerald Collins to the stand. Mr. Collins was a hefty man with a handlebar mustache.

"Please state your name sir."

"Gerald Collins."

"What is your profession?"

"I'm a ballistics specialist for the Scottsdale County sheriff's office."

"Did you do testing on the crime scene at Jessica Wilson's home in Scottsdale"?

"Yes, I did."

"Do you believe that Nicholas Wilson was shot while he was already

lying on the floor?"

"No, I do not."

"Please explain why."

"If Mr. Wilson had been lying on the terrazzo floor of Mrs. Wilson's home, the bullet would have nicked the floor when it exited his left ear. There were no bullet holes on the floor."

"What, in your opinion, was Nicholas Wilson doing when the third shot was fired?"

"I believe he was still standing up when he was shot in the back of the head."

"Thank you Mr. Collins. No further questions."

Hart declined to cross examine Collins and Collins was dismissed. When Hart called his next witness, I sat up straight. Joshua Swenson, looking quite handsome in a blue suit, walked up and took the stand. Jessica's eyes were wide and she bit her lip as she watched him. He wouldn't look at her. After he was sworn in, Hart began questioning him.

"Please tell us your name."

"Joshua Swenson."

"What is your profession?"

"I am a lawyer."

"How long have you know the defendant?"

"Two years."

"What was your relationship with her?"

"I dated her a year ago."

"Why did the relationship end?"

Joshua rolled his eyes. "I broke it off because Jessica Wilson is a disturbed woman."

Jessica's eyes narrowed and she glared at him. Doug Wilson leaned forward in his seat and nodded in agreement.

"How did Mrs. Wilson react when you ended the relationship?"

"She slit my tires and climbed up on my outdoor balcony and turned on the gas grill."

Several of the jurors gasped and one elderly juror shook her head and covered her mouth with her hand.

"How did you know it was her that did those things?"

"My neighbor witnessed it.'

"Was there anything else?'

"She kept calling me and screaming profanities at me. She wouldn't leave me alone."

"Were you afraid of her?"

"Yes, I was. I took out a restraining order on her."

"Did she leave you alone then?"

"Eventually. But I still look over my shoulder."

"Thank you Mr. Swenson. No further questions."

Meyers declined to cross examine. Although I had heard before the whole story about what Jessica had done to Josh, it was still rather shocking to hear him tell the Court about it. I hoped it would sway the jurors; so far, in my opinion, the police had botched their investigation rather badly!

The judge called for a 15 minute break. I stood up and stretched my legs. The room was buzzing with conversation and many people were speculating that Jessica would probably be called to the witness stand next. However, when Court resumed, Gabriel Meyer told the judge he was ready to rest his case and Hart said that he was also ready to do closing arguments. Many people were surprised that Jessica didn't get called to testify.

A reporter sitting next to me remarked to another reporter, "Is there anything she can add? Probably not."

Hart gave his closing arguments first. As he talked, Jessica cried. Hart told jurors that Jessica bought the gun, invited Nicholas to meet her that night and orchestrated the whole thing by going to the Scottsdale Police Station and claiming that Nicholas was going to kill her. He told them her motive was money and custody of the boys and he cited her bizarre behavior after Josh broke up with her as an example of her "unleashed fury."

"Do the right thing," he urged the jurors. "Jessica Wilson is a devious, cold-blooded killer who took her shot at trying to commit the perfect crime. She took the life of Nicholas Wilson deliberately in a well-planned of vengeance."

Meyers then went up and pounded on a podium while lambasting the police investigation. He said that Jessica was the victim of a violent and abusive man and that she had shot him in self-defense. He said that Jayson's testimony about seeing something in his father's hand proved that Nicholas had been holding a knife as he came at Jessica. He pointed out the casual, normal conversation she had had with Dr. Barnes, the plans to go out with Jimmy Fisher that night and the groceries that she left out as evidence that she had not planned the killing. He ended with saying, "I really believe in this case with all my heart."

The judge gave the jurors instructions and they filed out of the room, heading for the deliberation room. Jessica and her attorneys made a dramatic exit; again, she was acting like she was grief stricken and could hardly walk. The room and the spectators and news people talked amongst themselves, wondering how long the jury would be out and what the verdict would be. From what I overheard, most of them felt she was guilty. Nicholas's siblings talked quietly with each other and shunned reporters who tried to interview them. People milled around in the hall or outside to smoke or just get some air.

In just two hours, a bailiff came out and announced that the jury had reached a verdict. Anxiously, everybody scurried back into the courtroom and took their seats.

Jessica's face was pale and I could see perspiration on her forehead. The jury foreman stood up with a piece of paper in his hand. The judge asked him if they had reached a verdict.

"We have, Your Honor."

The bailiff walked over and took the paper from the foreman's hand and gave it to the judge, who read it with an impassive expression. Then he gave it back to the bailiff, who then took it back and handed it to the foreman.

"Please read the verdict sir." The judge instructed.

"We the jury find the defendant, Jessica Wilson, not guilty of murder in the first degree."

Instantly the courtroom burst into a cacophony of people talking excitedly, buzzing like a swarm of bees. Many people were shaking their heads. Jessica practically jumped up in the air and she hugged Atty, Meyers. The Wilson family members remained stone-faced but I could see tears in the eyes of Rosemary Wilson.

I was stunned. Listening to people on the way out of the door, I learned that most of them felt that the police had screwed up the investigation and I agreed wholeheartedly. I felt sick, disgusted and angry. Outside in front of the courthouse a few minutes later, Jessica was interviewed by a news reporter. I stood near enough so I could hear them talking but behind her slightly so she wouldn't see me.

"I just want to go home to my boys. I wasn't guilty and I'm glad the jury understood." She smiled radiantly through her tears. I felt like throwing up!

When asked why Jessica did not testify, Meyers, who stood next to her, said the question was "not appropriate" to prove that she shot in self-defense.

Jurors outside were questioned by the media. One man said, "I kind of knew from the questions they asked during the jury selection that they weren't going to put her through testifying for herself." According to him, deliberation began with a secret ballot. Ten voted "not guilty", two were undecided. Their discussion focused on Jayson's testimony. The jurors removed Nicholas's keys from the evidence bag and turned off the lights in the jury room. "They were not glary at all," one juror said.

Several of them blasted the police investigation and questioned why the knife was not tested for gunpowder, and why necessary materials such as string, was not brought to the crime scene. They said they examined photographs of Nicholas's hands during deliberation and saw gunpowder residue only on the lower portion of his palms, indicating that he "could have been" holding a knife. "One of the biggest things they didn't do was test the knife," said juror Hal Homer. "If there was gunpowder residue on the knife it would have proved he had it in his hand."

I drove home slowly that day, my head spinning. I didn't feel that justice had been done today. For the next few days I was physically and emotionally exhausted. I dragged myself to work and tried to keep up with Trevor and our schedules but it was hard. I talked to Freddie, Connie, and several other friends and everyone was upset that Jessica got off. Everyone who knew her felt she had literally "gotten away with murder". The news was full of details from the trial and I even heard Jessica was appearing on "Entertainment Tonight." I pretty much ignored most of the newspaper articles about the trial but one headline caught my attention.

TAXES WILL COVER WILSON'S EXPENSES

Cory Jones is an anxious man. The morning after a jury cleared Jessica Wilson of first-degree murder, Jones, the assistant county attorney responsible for paying court-appointed defense attorneys was on the phone with Gabriel Meyers' office. Jones pawed through the dog-eared, paperclipped pages of his law books and had good news for Meyers but bad news for the Scottsdale County taxpayers. All of Jessica Wilson's legal expenses, which will probably exceed $100,000 will be paid by taxpayers. Gabriel Meyers says that Mrs. Wilson lives "hand to mouth"; she doesn't have a dime.

"However, court records show otherwise. Between June 1 and March 30, Mrs. Wilson received about $17,481 from her ex-husband's estate to pay for expenses related to their children, the beneficiaries of the trust. During the same period, she and her boys received $20,430 in Social Security death benefits. She has also sued her ex-husbands estate, claiming that he owed her $67,000 in back alimony and child support. Mr. Wilson named his sons, Jayson and Brian, as beneficiaries of his life insurance policies, totaling nearly $1.1 million. Because the boys are minors, the estate will be managed by a trust. Nicholas Wilson's brother, Dr. William Wilson, is co-trustee.

"Wilson's brothers and sisters have declined to comment on the case or the verdict. Dr. Wilson said he wants the children to be well provided for, especially in terms of education, consistent with his brother's wishes. The trust has agreed to pay Jayson Wilson's tuition next year at a private school in Scottsdale.

"Without a job or place to live, Jessica Wilson has asked the trustees if she and her sons could live in Nicholas Wilson's condominium and the trustees agreed. Mrs. Wilson and her sons moved in. The trust paid $1,700 for moving, painting and cleaning expenses. New beds, bedding and a dining room table cost another $4,000, also paid by the trust. The trust pays nearly two-thirds of the utility bills and mortgage payment, nearly $2,000 for maintenance fees at the condo and the property taxes. Mrs. Wilson pays $233 a month in rent. She receives a monthly stipend of $400. In addition, the trust pays for the children's clothing, medical needs, bicycles, camp tuition and entertainment expenses. The day after the jury found Jessica Wilson innocent, Atty. Gabriel Meyers' office called the bank managed the trust to ask for $1,000 so that Jessica could take her children to Disneyland. The trust agreed to give her $600. "The children's money clearly needs to be spent in ways that benefit them," Dr. Wilson said. "We know the kids have had a hard time lately; they could use a day at Disneyland."

What a travesty, I thought. It all literally made me sick. Two days later, another article jumped out at me.

ESTATE, WIFE SETTLE SUITS OVER DEATH

Jessica Wilson's legal woes are over. She has settled her legal Complaints with the $1 Million estate of Nicholas Wilson. Under Terms of the Feb. 15th settlement, the estate agreed to pay her $23,500. The insurance company that carries the homeowners' policy on the Scottsdale home where Nicholas Wilson died will pay the estate $20,000. Also, Jessica Wilson will receive evidence from the criminal case, including the .357 Magnum she used to shoot and kill Nicholas Wilson and the 8 inch knife found in his hand.

James Wilson's wallet, two gold chains and the watch he was wearing when he died will be given to his family.

CHAPTER NINETEEN

A Day at the Beach

A few weeks after Jessica's trial, Trevor's school held its' annual "white elephant" auction, a fundraiser for the school's arts program. I had read in the paper that Jessica and her boys had gone to Disneyland so I decided to attend the auction. Jessica had sent me a note, asking me to call her, but I threw it away. I was still quite annoyed about the way the trial went down; I truly believed, in my gut, that she had gotten away with murder.

It was a beautiful, sunny day. Trevor and I pulled into the parking lot full of BMWs, Jaguars, Rolls Royces and even a couple of limousines. A stream of people were walking towards the field next to the school and we followed them. Tables were covered with gold fabric displaying the items people had donated, such as exquisite vases, picture frames, oriental rugs, jewelry and even a computer. My parents had donated an almost new set of golf clubs.

Trevor and I stopped at a refreshment table for some lemonade and cookies. I could hear people discussing their most recent vacations, to Hawaii,

France and other exotic locations. I envied them and wished I could take a vacation. As I was looking around, a woman in a red dress caught my eye and it took me a second to realize it was Jessica! I grabbed Trevor by the arm and pulled him behind a tree.

"Mom! Quit it! What's wrong with you?" he complained as he rubbed his arm.

"Shh, don't move. Jessica is here." My heart was thumping and I felt like kicking the tree. Shit! I'd thought she would still be at Disneyland. "Mom, I want to go see Jayson and Brian."

"No, I'm sorry but no, we can't."

"Come on . . . ."

"No Trevor, absolutely not!" I peeked around the tree and saw that Jessica was talking to some people. I decided the best way to avoid her was to cut through the school building, then head to the car. We made it into the school and we passed Trevor's art classroom.

"Mom, mom! Come here, just a minute, please!" He stopped me. Let's go into my class. I want to show you my project."

"Sure honey." As long as I didn't have to talk to Jessica, I didn't care what we did. We walked into the deserted art room. Every inch of wall space was covered with artwork done by the kids. Trevor showed me his sketch of a giraffe. I was really impressed; he definitely had talent. We walked around, looking at a few of the other drawings. I stopped short when I came to a watercolor picture labeled, "Self Portrait by

Jayson Wilson ". It was a bizarre and disturbing painting of a face with eyes that were crazily glazed. Dark scribbles and blots of red paint around the head brought to mind a tortured and frightened soul. It made me deeply sad. I led Trevor out to the car and we left as fast as I could drive. But the picture stayed in my mind; Jayson and Brian Wilson were the real victims.

The following Saturday I dropped Trevor off to meet some of his friends at the roller skating rink, then I drove to a small, man-made lake a few miles away and found a quiet spot on the cinnamon-colored sand, away from the other sun-worship A few sun-tanned tourists trudged past me, loaded with wet towels, beach bags and bottled water. I was still emotionally spent from the stress of the whole situation with Jessica. I ran to the water and the hot, foamy waves covered my feet. The healing elixir of water and sun were just what I needed, I walked out against the small waves until only the tips of my toes reached the bottom of the lake, then I floated on my back, smiling. I felt more peaceful and calm than I had in a very long time. A loud splash startled me, covering my face with water. I sputtered and struggled to stand up.

"Judy!" A familiar voice grated my nerves and I wiped the water out of my eyes and face.

Jessica Wilson was standing just a few feet away from me! She had a strange expression on her face; it was a cross between a smile and a grimace.

"I was yelling at you Judy! Didn't you hear me?

Filled with dread and anxiety, I tried to find my voice. "No, I didn't Jessica."

"You've been avoiding me again." She inched closer. I backed up and realized that there was a drop off right behind me where the water became very deep. "Why didn't you ever call me? Didn't you get my note?" She kept coming closer. I glanced at the people on the shore, hoping someone would see us. But they all seemed oblivious to my situation.

"Jessica, I've told you before. Your life is too disturbing for me."

I started dog-paddling, trying to swim around her, but she kept blocking my path. Panic began to set in and I was becoming tired.

"You know, I heard some nasty rumors about people saying I planned to kill Nicholas."

"Well you got off, didn't you? I wouldn't worry about rumors."

"As a matter of fact, Judy, I heard that you were one of the people behind the rumors!"

"I need you to move Jessica. I'm getting tired." I was short of breath.

She was just inches away from me now. "I don't care. I'd kill him again in a heartbeat!"

There was a crazy gleam in her eyes.

"Jessica, you can't mean that!"

"The hell I don't!" She screamed. "It felt great Judy, firing my gun at that bastard! It was wonderful . . . better than sex! I just wish I'd done it sooner. He had it coming!"

Fear and adrenaline kicked in and gave me the energy to plunge through the water around her and I started swimming towards the shore. She dove under the water and came up next to me.

Laughing, she grabbed me by the hair and pushed my head under the water! Pure terror overcame me as the water filled my nose and mouth. I managed to pull away from her and break the surface of the ocean.

"Come on Judy. Let's play!" She dove towards me again but fury unleashed inside of me like power I had never felt before and I shoved her hard, back against the waves. I quickly dove in and swam to shore, with Jessica right on my heels. I managed to stumble to my blanket and collapse. My heart was racing and I took deep breaths as I wrapped a towel around my shivering arms. Jessica got out and sauntered over and sat next to me. She opened her beach bag and rummaged through it, "Don't worry Judy," she said casually, as if nothing strange had just happened. "I'm leaving town for good soon. I need to get away from here and all the people who judge me." She pulled a gun out of the bag and laughed. "I made out pretty good, didn't I? See . . . I even got my gun back . . . minus three bullets!!"

I shook my head and gathered my things. I had reached the saturation point with Jessica; I just didn't give a damn anymore. The sky was starting to cloud over. It was definitely time for me to split. Another day ruined by Jessica.

"Goodbye Jessica. And good luck."

"Judy!" she yelled. "Be careful! Looks like a wind is picking up. Might be a storm!"

I turned at glared at her for a long time, then said, "Jessica, *I AM THE STORM*

The End

ABOUT THE AUTHOR

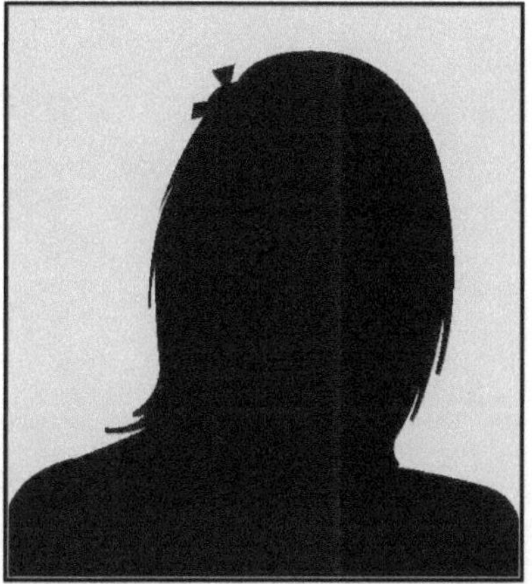

This is where the author biography text goes.